# The Secret Country

Chapter illustrations
by Adam Stower

BOOK I

# The Secret Country

## THE EIDOLON CHRONICLES

## JANE JOHNSON

Simon & Schuster Books for Young Readers
New York   London   Toronto   Sydney

SIMON & SCHUSTER BOOKS FOR YOUNG READERS
An imprint of Simon & Schuster Children's Publishing Division
1230 Avenue of the Americas, New York, New York 10020
This book is a work of fiction. Any references to historical events, real people, or real locales are used fictitiously. Other names, characters, places, and incidents are products of the author's imagination, and any resemblance to actual events or locales or persons, living or dead, is entirely coincidental.
Copyright © 2005 by Jane Johnson
Illustrations copyright © 2005 by Adam Stower
Originally published in Great Britain in 2005 by Simon and Schuster UK Ltd
First U.S. edition, 2006
All rights reserved, including the right of reproduction in whole or in part in any form.
SIMON & SCHUSTER BOOKS FOR YOUNG READERS is a trademark of Simon & Schuster, Inc.
Book design by Einav Aviram
The text for this book is set in Adobe Garamond.
Manufactured in the United States of America
2 4 6 8 10 9 7 5 3 1
Library of Congress Cataloging-in-Publication Data
Johnson, Jane.
The secret country / Jane Johnson ; chapter illustrations by Adam Stower.—1st U.S. ed.
p. cm.
Summary: Having learned from a talking cat that he and his sisters are the half-elfin royalty of a parallel world called Eidolon, twelve-year-old Ben Arnold attempts to stop his evil uncle from smuggling magical creatures between the two worlds to sell on the black market.
ISBN-13: 978-1-4169-0712-1
ISBN-10: 1-4169-0712-2
[1. Magic—Fiction. 2. Cats—Fiction. 3. Animals, Mythical—Fiction. 4. Space and time—Fiction. 5. England—Fiction. 6. Fantasy—Fiction.] I. Stower, Adam, ill. II. Title.
PZ7.J632158Sec 2006
[Fic]—dc22
2005004449

*For William*

# Contents

# Part One
## Here

*Advertisement in*
**Horse & Hunt** *magazine:*

Searching for something more sporting than a fox to chase? We can offer your Hunt the opportunity to pursue more challenging game. If you have ever dreamed of killing a direwolf, saber-toothed tiger, or the legendary cameleopard, we can make your dreams come true. Why spend hours pursuing a pathetic, defenseless creature across other people's land, when you could have something really exciting to boast about? Write to us at: WonderFinders Incorporated, PO Box 721, Bixbury, Oxon OX7 9HP. All correspondence dealt with in complete secrecy and confidence. Waste no time—these creatures are rare, and you could make them rarer still!

## Chapter One

# Mr. Dodds's Pet Emporium

Ben Arnold was not a remarkable-looking boy. Not unless you looked closely. He had unruly straw-blond hair, thin legs, and quite large feet. But his eyes had a faraway expression; and when you got close enough to notice, you could see that while the left one was a sensible hazel brown, the right shone a wild and vivid green. Ben believed this oddness to be the result of a childhood accident. One day, his mother had told him, while being pushed up the High Street in his stroller he had stuck his head out unexpectedly and banged it hard on a lamppost. He had been rushed to the hospital and when he came out one brown eye had gone green. It was as simple as that. Ben couldn't actually remember the accident, but he had long since stopped wondering about it. He had other things on his mind, after all.

Which was why, this Saturday morning, he found himself walking briskly along Quinx Lane, his heart thumping with excitement. It had taken him weeks to save up for this. One day on his way home from school, when pressing his nose up against the glass of Mr. Dodds's Pet Emporium, he had seen something so special he had been obsessed ever since. Amongst all the colorful paraphernalia of the Pet Emporium, looking as wicked and shiny as jewels, switching back and forth in their brightly lit tank, their fins fluttering like the pennants on a medieval knight's lance, were two Rare Mongolian Fighting Fish, as a neon-orange cardboard sign announced. Did they live up to their name? he wondered; and if so, how did fish fight? He had taken a deep breath and gone into the shop there and then to ask how much they cost. He had nearly fainted on the spot when Mr. Dodds told him, and so had headed home, grim and silent with determination, moneymaking schemes careering round his head.

Every day since, he had checked to make sure the fish were still there. He wanted to own them more than he had wanted anything in his life.

Mongolian Fighting Fish!

He desired them. He coveted them, a word for which he had had till then only the vaguest of Biblical associations. Before he went to sleep each night, he pictured them swimming around in a tank mysterious with soft light and fronds of weed. When he slept, they swam through his dreams.

He'd saved his birthday money (twelve at last!), his pocket money, and whatever he could make from extra errands and odd jobs. He'd cleaned his father's car (three times, though it was an ancient Morris, and polishing it just seemed to expose the rust patches); he'd mowed next door's lawn (and a flowerbed, when the mower got out of control, but luckily they hadn't seemed to notice); he'd peeled potatoes and washed windows; he'd vacuumed and dusted and ironed, and even (and this had been *really* horrible) changed his youngest sister's diaper, which made his mother very happy indeed.

Before long, he'd gathered quite a tidy sum, which he carried around with him, to keep his elder sister off it.

"I can tell it's burning a hole in your pocket!" his mother had teased him gently.

What would happen, he wondered, if it *did* burn a hole in his pocket? Once it had done that, would it stop at his leg? Or would it keep on burning, right through his leg, into the road, down through the sewers and into the core of the Earth? Goodness knows what might happen if he didn't buy his fish: Failure to do so might bring about the end of the world!

He turned off the High Street and into Quinx Lane; and there it was, squeezed between Waitrose and Boots the Chemist. The great ornate gold letters above the shopfront announced it grandly: Mr. Dodds's Pet Emporium. A throwback from a bygone age, his father called it, and Ben sort of knew what he meant without being able to put it into words. It was a shop full of clutter and oddities. It was a shop full of wonders and weirdness. You never knew what you might step on next: in amongst the shiny silver cages, the collars and leashes and squeaky toys, the dog baskets and cat hammocks, the sawdust and sunflower seeds, the hamsters and talking birds, the lizards and Labrador puppies, you had a vague feeling you might just stumble upon a tangle of tarantulas, a nest of scorpions, a sleeping gryphon, or a giant sloth. (He'd never yet done so, but he lived in hope.)

Holding his breath, Ben gazed in through the murky window. They were still there, at the back of the shop: his Mongolian Fighting Fish—swimming around without a care in the world, little realizing that today their lives would change forever. For today they would be leaving Mr. Dodds's Pet Emporium and traveling—in the finest plastic bag money could buy—all the way to Ben's bedroom, First Door on the Right on the Upstairs Landing, Gray Havens, 27 Underhill Road, just past the Number 17 bus stop. And that afternoon Awful Uncle Aleister was coming over to drop off an old fish tank for which they no longer had a use. ("Awful" had become an automatic part of his name as far as Ben was concerned, for very many reasons not unrelated to his braying laugh, loud voice, and complete insensitivity; and the fact that he and Aunt Sybil had spawned his loathed cousin, Cynthia.)

Feeling the weight of destiny in his hands, Ben pushed open the heavy brassbound door. At once he was assailed by noise: cheeps and squawks and scratchings; rustlings and snores and barks. It was really quite alarming. Thank goodness, he thought suddenly, that fish were quiet. Surely even Mongolian Fighting Fish couldn't make much noise? A badly behaved pet would be a terrible trial to his poor mother, as Aunt Sybil had reminded him. Frequently. And she did have a point; for Cynthia's piranhas had not been the best behaved of creature companions. But that was another story.

Ben's mother had not been well for some time now. She had complained of tiredness and headaches, and the skin below her eyes was always thin and dark. No one knew what was the matter with her, and she just seemed to get worse and worse. She had, as Ben's father said, always been "delicate"; but in the last few weeks she had declined suddenly, and now she found it easier to use a wheelchair than to walk. It made Ben very sad to see how tenderly his father picked her up at night to carry her to their room.

Sometimes Ben would find his father sitting quietly at the kitchen table with his head in his hands.

"It's as if she's allergic to the whole world," he had once said helplessly.

But she wasn't allergic to animals. Ben's mother loved animals. She had, as people say, a way with them. Stray cats came to her as if from nowhere. Dogs walked up to her in the street and laid their heads in her hands. Birds would settle on the ground in front of her. Ben had even seen a pigeon land upon her shoulder, as if it had something to tell her. She had encouraged him to save for the fish. "Looking after other creatures teaches us responsibility," she had said. "It's good to care about someone other than yourself."

A man pushed in front of Ben, and for a moment he was terribly afraid that he would stride up to the counter and demand that Mr. Dodds's assistant pack up Ben's fish; but instead he grabbed a sack of dried dog food, slapped a ten-pound note on the counter, and left without even waiting for his change. Outside the shop, its thick leash tied very thoroughly to the brass rail, a huge black dog glared at the man, its red jaws dripping saliva onto the pavement. Anxiously, Ben stepped over a heap of spilled straw, avoided a collection of oddly shaped and buckled tartan coats, threaded his way between a narrow row of cages, one of which contained a noisy black bird with orange eyes, and—

Stopped.

He tried to step forward a pace, but something—someone?—was holding him back. He stared around, but there was no sign of anyone behind him. Shaking his head, he started off again. But again he was pulled back. He must have snagged his jacket on one of the cages.

He turned around carefully so as not to make the snag any worse. It would not do to return home with a pair of Mongolian Fighting Fish and a ripped coat. He fiddled with the area that seemed to be caught, and found, not a spike of wire or a sharp catch, but something warm and furry and yet hard as iron. Skewing his head around until his neck hurt, he stared down. It was a cat. A small black and brown cat with shiny gold eyes and a remarkably determined arm. It appeared to have reached out of its cage and snagged its sharp little claws in his jacket. He smiled. How sweet! He made an attempt to pry it loose, but the cat clamped its fist together even harder. The fabric of Ben's jacket became rucked and furrowed. Ben's smile became a frown.

"Let go!" he said under his breath, picking at its powerful claws.

The cat looked at him, unblinking. Then it said very distinctly, in a voice as harsh and gravelly as that of any private investigator with a bad smoking habit, "There's no way you're leaving this shop without me, sonny."

Ben was shocked. He stared at the cat. Then he stared around the shop. Had anyone else heard this exchange, or was he daydreaming? But the other customers all appeared to be getting on with their business—inspecting piles of hamsters sleeping thoughtlessly on each other's heads; poking sticks at the parrot to try to make it say something outrageous; buying a dozen live mice to feed to their python . . .

He turned back to the cat. It was still watching him in its disconcerting way. He began to wonder whether it actually had eyelids or was just saving energy. Perhaps he was going mad. To test the theory he said, "My name is Ben, not Sonny."

"I know," said the cat.

## Chapter Two

# A Sudden Change of Heart

"I came here to buy some fish," Ben said firmly. "Mongolian Fighting Fish." The cat still hadn't blinked. "Over there, see."

The cat's eyes flicked boredly across the bank of glass tanks on the far wall of the shop. It still held on to his jacket tightly. "Oh, fish," it said. "You don't want fish. Who wants wet pets?"

"I do," Ben protested hotly. "I've been saving up for them for weeks."

"But what can fish *do*?" said the cat in a tone of ultimate reason. "They just swim up and down all day." It thought for a moment. "And sometimes they die and float to the surface. It's not a lot to boast about. It isn't as if they have much effect upon the world."

"These," said Ben proudly, as if he owned them already, "are Mongolian Fighting Fish. They . . . fight."

The cat regarded him askance. He could have sworn it raised an eyebrow, but because cats' faces have fur all over and not just as eyebrows, it was hard to tell.

"Obviously," the beast said, this time with a clear edge of contempt, "you know very little about fish. Mongolian Fighting Fish indeed. There's no such thing. It's just a marketing strategy. So many pretty fish to choose from: How do you persuade a boy to part with his hard-earned cash? You give your fish an exciting name and let your customer's imagination run away with itself."

At last it blinked.

Ben was furious. "That's not true! I saw a picture of them in *Fish: The Ultimate Encyclopedia*—"

"And who was the author of that esteemed tome?"

Ben concentrated hard. He pictured the cover of the book, with its gorgeous angelfish and archerfish, its dogfish and catfish and rabbitfish, thornbacks and triggerfish, its groupers and gobies and grunions. And in the middle of them all, swimming in a sea of fins and scales in long black letters as sleek as any shark, the name A. E. Dodds . . .

His face fell.

"You mean, it's a trick?"

The little cat nodded. "Worst sort of untruth." It eyed him solemnly. "Mongolia's landlocked and mainly desert, anyway. Nowhere for a fish to live."

"Next you'll be telling me they don't fight, either."

The cat shrugged. "They might argue a bit, I suppose."

A shadow fell across him.

"I beg your pardon, laddie," the shadow said. "What don't fight?"

Ben looked up. Mr. Dodds was standing in front of him. Or possibly, since he was a very tall man, looming over him. He didn't look as you might expect the owner of a pet emporium to look. He wasn't old and benign-looking, and he didn't wear overalls covered with dog hair. He didn't have little half-moon spectacles, or smell of rabbit food. No, Mr. Dodds wore a sharply cut Italian suit with narrow lapels and very shiny buttons. He had a bowtie made from some sort of weirdly patterned fur, like luminous leopard-skin, and his smile was as white as a television advertisement for toothpaste.

Ben quailed slightly. Mr. Dodds had that sort of effect on you.

"Er, the Mongolian Fighting Fish?"

"Nonsense, laddie! They fight like demons. Not in here, of course—too many distractions; but get them home to a nice quiet room and they'll be at each other's throat in no time. Lovely family pets."

Ben was beginning to have serious doubts about his dreams of the last several weeks. Even if Mr. Dodds was truthful, the idea of owning a pair of fish that actually wanted to hurt one another was becoming less attractive by the minute. Bravely, he looked the pet shop owner in the eye. Mr. Dodds had large eyes, eyes so dark they seemed to be all pupil and no iris, as if all available light were being sucked into them with not even the slightest hint of a reflection.

"I had heard," Ben started nervously, "that some creatures don't always live up to their names. And also," he went on quickly, "that Mongolia has no ocean, and therefore no . . . fish. . . ."

Mr. Dodds' eyes widened slightly. A second later and his smile followed suit, but the expression that had crept onto his face was not amused.

"And who might have given you this remarkable information, laddie?" he inquired gently.

Ben looked down.

"Well, go on then, Ben," came the gravelly voice of the cat, "tell him who told you." It grinned at him unhelpfully.

Ben looked up and found Mr. Dodds fixing the cat with a gimlet glare, a glare that suggested he would like to strangle it, or maybe just swallow it down, fur and all, in a single mouthful. Even so, it was hard to tell whether he had been a party to their conversation, or just wasn't very fond of this particular item of stock.

"Er," floundered Ben, "I can't remember. Maybe I read it in a book."

"Oh, yes," said the cat sarcastically. "That would be Mr. Dodds's *Great Big Book of Lies*, then, would it?"

The pet shop owner reached out with sudden shocking speed and did something that made the cat wail. Ben whirled round in horror, only to find Mr.

Dodds extricating the creature's claws, with seeming care, from the back of Ben's jacket.

"Whoopsadaisy," Mr. Dodds said lightly. "This little fellow seems to have got himself caught up with you."

So saying, he gave the final claw a spiteful twist and pushed the cat away with an uncompromising finger. It hissed at him, ears laid flat against its skull, and retreated into the cage.

Mr. Dodds straightened up. He seemed taller than ever.

"You've got to go with your heart, laddie, follow your heart's desire. It does no good to hanker after a dream and not pursue it to the ends of the earth." He leered at Ben, gave him an encouraging wink. "Do the right thing, son: Spend the money you've saved all these weeks. Can't have it burning a hole in your pocket, can we?" He moved toward the fish tanks, reached up to collect the little plastic scoop to remove the Mongolian Fighting Fish, and regarded Ben expectantly.

Ben looked at the black and brown cat. It was crouched at the back of the cage with its paw cradled to its chest. When it looked back at him, its eyes were hot with misery, and at the same time a barely suppressed fury. He sensed a challenge, an invitation. He looked at the fish. They circled sweetly through the miniature bridge with which someone had decorated their tank, entirely unconcerned by the world and its ways. One of them swam up to the surface, the artificial lighting making its scales glow like rubies and sapphires, and banged its head on the air pipe. They were, he decided, very pretty, but possibly not very bright. He looked back at Mr. Dodds—who was standing there like a waiter in a posh restaurant, fish tank lid in one hand, scoop in the other, ready to dish out his order—and made a momentous decision.

"How much for the cat?" he asked.

Mr. Dodds was not to be deterred. "That little beast's not a suitable pet for a nice boy like you, laddie. Vile temper it's got."

From the cage behind him came a hiss.

"Don't believe a word he says." The cat was sitting at the front of the cage, grasping the bars with its paws. "I've never bitten anyone." It paused, then growled, "Well, no one that didn't deserve to be bitten." It gave Mr. Dodds a hard look, then turned imploring eyes to Ben. "You have to get me out of here—"

A heavy hand fell on Ben's shoulder. He looked up to find the pet shop owner beaming at him benevolently. It was an unsettling sight. "Tell you what, laddie," said Mr. Dodds, drawing Ben away from the cat's cage. "I'll do you a special deal on the fish: two for the price of one—how's that? Can't say fairer, can I? Mind you, I'll go out of business if I keep letting my better nature get in the way!" The beam became a full, open grin. Mr. Dodds's teeth were remarkably sharp, Ben noticed: more like a dog's teeth than a human's. Or even a shark's . . .

"No, sir, Mr. Dodds, I've changed my mind. I don't want the fish anymore, I want the cat. It's"—he searched for a persuasive description—"really pretty."

"*Pretty?*" The cat fairly squawked with indignation. "You might leave a chap a bit of dignity! Pretty, indeed. Bast's teeth! How'd you like it if I called you pretty, eh?"

Mr. Dodds was frowning now, and his polite smile looked less than sincere. "Sorry, laddie, but you can't have the cat," he said through gritted teeth. "I've promised it elsewhere, and that's that."

"It hasn't got a sold sign on it," Ben pointed out reasonably.

The pet shop owner leaned toward him, his face dark with blood. "Now look here, laddie: This is my shop and I shall sell my stock to whomsoever I please. And I do not please to sell you this cat. All right?"

A terrible wail came from behind them. Everyone in the shop stopped what they were doing and stared. The cat was writhing around the cage, clutching its stomach and howling bloody murder. Ben ran to the side of the cage.

"What's wrong?"

The little cat winked at him. "Don't worry, I've a few tricks of my own up my fur. . . ." Its voice rose in an earsplitting shriek.

Mr. Dodds glowered down at it. Then he bent down till his face was on a level with the cat's and said quietly to it, "Don't think this will save you. I know your game."

A young woman carrying a baby in the crook of her arm looked very shocked at this hard-heartedness. She whispered something to her husband, who tapped Mr. Dodds on the shoulder.

"Excuse me," said the man, "the kitten doesn't look very well. Shouldn't you be doing something for it?"

Mr. Dodds gave the man an oily, but forbidding, smile. "Terrible little playactor, this cat," he said. "It'd do anything for a bit of attention."

A big, elderly lady with colored spectacles bustled up and joined in. "Nonsense!" she cried. "Poor little thing. Animals always know when there's something wrong with them." She stuck a pudgy finger through the bars. The cat rolled weakly onto its side and nudged its head against her hand. "Aaaah," she said. "They always know when a human is their best chance of survival too."

Ben saw his chance. "I want to buy it and take it to the vet's," he said loudly. "But he won't let me— keeps trying to sell me some expensive fish instead."

Quite a crowd had gathered around them now and there was a lot of muttering and shaking of heads. Mr. Dodds looked angry and beset. The cat flashed Ben a knowing look.

"Oh, all right then," Mr. Dodds said at last, gritting those terrible teeth. He smiled around at the crowd, then dropped an avuncular hand back onto Ben's shoulder. Ben could feel the man's fingernails biting into the skin beneath his jacket. They felt as hard and horny as claws. "Have the creature, then."

When the other customers had drifted out of earshot, Mr. Dodds named his price. Not only did it include all the money Ben had saved for the Mongolian Fighting Fish, it also meant handing over his bus fare. Mr. Dodds took it of him with very bad grace and stomped off into the back of the shop to fetch a cardboard carrier. Ben leaned down to the cat. "I've no idea what's going on here," he said as sternly as he could manage. "So as soon as we're out of here you've got some explaining to do. It's taken me weeks to save that cash, and I don't know what my parents will say when I come back with a talking cat and no fish."

The cat rolled its eyes. "Just regard it as the first step to saving the world, okay? If it makes you feel any better. Now here he comes, so shut up and behave like a grateful customer."

Ben did as he was told so well that in the end Mr. Dodds felt obliged to give him two free cans of cat food—"as a goodwill gesture"—and two minutes later Ben was out in the street with a cardboard box in his arms and the two cans balancing precariously on the top. As he walked slowly down Quinx Lane, Ben could feel Mr. Dodds's eyes boring into his back until he turned the corner onto the High Street, where the bustle of traffic and shoppers made the last half hour feel even more bizarre. Ben was beginning to think he had experienced some sort of fit or waking dream when the box spoke to him.

"Thank you, Ben," it said, and the unmistakable, gravelly voice was solemn. "You have, literally, saved my life."

Ben held the box away from him so that he could peer in through the airholes. As if in response, a small pink muzzle emerged, sniffed once or twice, and withdrew again.

"You *can* talk, then," Ben breathed. "I thought I might have been imagining it."

"Everything talks, Ben," the cat said enigmatically, "but it's not everyone who can hear."

## Chapter Three

# Cynthia's Piranhas

Gray Havens, 27 Underhill Road, was an unremarkable semi-detached house in a long row of other unremarkable semi-detached houses on the outskirts of town, but Ben loved it. Always warm in the winter and cool in the summer, it was filled with comfortable furniture and secret, dusty nooks and crannies; and out in the back garden there grew the largest apple tree he had ever seen, a tree that produced hundreds of delicious green-and-red apples every summer and still had the generosity to let him climb into its branches and build a tree house. He had lived at Gray Havens all his life, and it usually made his heart lift when he rounded the corner by the soccer pitch and caught sight of his home. Today, though, as he plodded up Parsonage Road and turned into Underhill Road, his heart sank; for there, in front of his own house, and blocking the driveway to Number 28, was Uncle Aleister's gleaming black Jaguar car.

"Oh, no," breathed Ben unhappily.

Ben was not fond of his mother's awful brother, or Uncle Aleister's wife, Sybil. And he was especially not fond of their daughter, the awful Cynthia. They lived on the other side of town, past Aldstane Park, on one of the new "executive" estates: huge houses masquerading as genuine Tudor mansions, with lawns like smooth green carpets and flowers that grew exactly when and where they were supposed to. There was never a weed to be seen at Awful Uncle Aleister's: No weed would dare to spoil that perfect symmetry. Everything in the house looked brand-new—bright white carpets and pale pink leather sofas and armchairs—as if the plastic wrappings had just been whisked off as you rang the bell (which played a fetching version of "Greensleeves"). Ben's mum often muttered darkly that she thought that was exactly what Aunt Sybil did, for she couldn't for the life of her understand how anyone could keep such a color scheme so immaculate and still live there like a proper family. There was none of the comfortable clutter you would find at their house—newspapers and books, packets of cookies, half-finished drawings, games and postcards, and bits of wood or pebbles they had collected on their walks. No, at Uncle Aleister's house you sat awkwardly on the edge of the sofa (unless it was a particularly hot day and Aunt Sybil suggested she put a cloth down first, in case you sweated into the leather) and clutched your glass of bitter grapefruit juice and stayed silent while the adults made polite small talk, which mainly consisted of Uncle Aleister puffing on a fat cigar and boasting about how he'd made yet another fabulous sum of money on one of his deals. ("That sort of money," Ben's father would say, once they were back in their car, "could only possibly come from someone else's misery." And though Ben had no idea what sort of job his uncle had, he would nod his head sagely.)

The other torment of visiting their relatives was being made to accompany Cousin Cynthia upstairs to see her latest acquisition.

The last time it had been piranhas.

Cynthia never seemed to have normal pets. Or rather, if she did, they never seemed to last long. She had once had a very playful collie puppy, but it had mysteriously disappeared the day after it bit her. Her rabbit had made a successful bid for freedom by tunneling out of its run in the backyard; her tarantula appeared to have committed suicide by hurling itself in front of Uncle Aleister's Jaguar; and the boa constrictor she had had the previous year was last seen disappearing down the toilet. The piranhas, though, were something else.

There had been eight of them to begin with: ugly little brutes with bad overbites and overlapping teeth. Cousin Cynthia—a painfully thin girl with green eyes and mean elbows—had invited Ben and his sister Ellie round for tea to show them off. "Look!" she had cried, gleefully dangling a goldfish over the tank. (The goldfish was the last remaining one of six she had "won" from a local fair.) The goldfish had rolled its eyes and struggled: It knew what was coming next. Ben was appalled. He stared at Cynthia, his mouth open in protest, but before he could stop her, she had smiled and dropped the goldfish, and when he looked down, the water in the tank was murky and churned.

When at last the water cleared, there was no sign of the goldfish; but oddly enough, there seemed to be fewer piranhas, too.

Ben counted them. It was difficult, since they kept trying to confuse him by swimming around, but he stuck at it. One, two, three, four, five, six . . . seven . . . He counted them again. Still seven. Definitely only seven. The eighth had vanished along with the goldfish. The remaining piranhas stared back at him blankly as if to say, "Well, what did you expect? We're piranhas, after all." After this, he'd quite gone off the idea of fish-and-chips for tea and had mumbled his excuses and gone home. By the weekend there had been only one piranha left, as Cynthia cheerfully confided to him at school. One great big, very satisfied-looking piranha.

And then, she told him, it got so hungry that it ate itself.

Ben could never quite work that one out; but since it was the tank it had occupied that Uncle Aleister was going to be installing in Ben's bedroom as a home for his new Mongolian Fighting Fish, it was clear that Cousin Cynthia's last piranha no longer had a use for it.

He walked down the road slowly, not looking forward to explaining that he no longer needed the tank. When he arrived home, he put the box down carefully outside the front door. "I won't be long," he said softly. "Just stay here and don't make any noise."

He could smell Awful Uncle Aleister's cigar smoke even before he opened the door; and as soon as he did, an awful laugh rang out. For one wonderful moment Ben thought that maybe he'd come around to say Ben couldn't have the fish tank after all. But no: He opened the door, only to hear his uncle exclaiming, "Marvelous tank that, Clive." (This being Ben's father.) "Top of the range. If it could hold all those piranhas, I'm sure it can manage two tiny little Siamese Dancing Fish."

"Mongolian Fighting Fish," Ben amended automatically.

Uncle Aleister turned around and glowered at him through a cloud of smoke, but since Uncle Aleister had huge black eyebrows that almost joined in the middle to make one great furry caterpillar of an eye-brow, it could be quite hard to tell when he wasn't glowering. "Don't you know it's not polite to contra-dict your elders and betters, Benny?"

"But . . . ," Ben started, only to go quiet when his father shook his head at him. "Yes, sir."

"Come along then, Benny," Awful Uncle Aleister said benevolently, taking him firmly by the shoulder and leading him back out into the hall. "Let me show you the beautiful tank your father and I have just spent two happy hours installing for you, a tank in which your fish can dance their little hearts out."

Ben stared helplessly back over his shoulder at his father, who, shielded by Uncle Aleister's back, was rolling his eyes heavenward. "Up you go, son," he said. "We've done a lovely job."

They had. The tank was exactly where Ben had imagined it, on top of the chest of drawers and in front of the window, so that the afternoon light played through the emerald green weed and lit each air bubble that issued from the complex filtration unit to a perfect silvery sphere.

"That's, ah, amazing," he said at last.

Uncle Aleister beamed. "Isn't it just? And a proper

bargain for you, Benny, since it cost the best part of three hundred pounds only last Christmas. Your father's kindly agreed to come and trim our hedges in exchange. Marvelous with his hands, your father.' He ruffled Ben's hair, a gesture Ben particularly hated, but not as much as he hated being called Benny. "So talented. I always say to him if working with your hands was as highly valued as running a successful import business, then it'd be him who was a millionaire living in King Henry Close, and me who'd be living here in this dreadful hovel. Ha-ha!" His uncle's awful laugh rolled out round the room and Ben's father, appearing suddenly at the door, smiled weakly.

"Well, where are your fish, then, son?" he asked, to get Aleister off his favorite topic of conversation. "Let's see how they like their new home, shall we?"

Ben was stumped. He couldn't think of a word to say or a thing to do. Instead he mumbled something inaudible and fled downstairs in panic. Not only would Uncle Aleister kill him for causing him so much needless bother, but his poor father would have to spend hours working in the garden at King Henry Close, with Awful Auntie Sybil flapping around him and asking, "Please, Clive, not to trample the grass . . ."

At the foot of the stairs Ben's mother appeared, silently, as if by magic. Her new wheelchair was remarkably free of squeaks and squeals. She was a small, tired-looking woman, with pale gold hair and lively eyes, and in her arms she carried Ben's tiny little sister, Alice. By now Ben had just started working on his best excuses for arriving home without the fish: Someone had stolen them right out of his hands outside the pet shop? The fish had somehow contracted a rare disease and weren't well enough to travel? The pet shop had sold out of Mongolian Fighting Fish and were going to have to send to Mongolia to get some more, which could take at least six months? . . . He was concentrating so hard he almost tripped over the wheelchair.

"Oops, sorry, Mum!"

In reply, his mother dropped him a long, slow wink. She did this sort of thing from time to time, and Ben wasn't entirely sure what she meant by it, though it always made him feel as if she could see right through him, into the very depths of his soul. It was useless trying to lie to her.

Even so, he couldn't imagine she'd welcome the addition of a cat to the household. Still racking his brains, he opened the front door.

The cardboard box was exactly where he had left it, but someone had artfully placed a transparent plastic bag in the middle of the doorstep. The bag was ripped and water was puddling around it and dripping off the step, where it ran in a long thin runnel down the garden path. At the end of the path, a big ginger tomcat sat licking its paws thoughtfully. Ben wrinkled his forehead. What on earth was going on?

"Don't say a word." The voice came from very close to the ground. "Just look upset. Everything will be fine."

Ben knelt down to interrogate the box further, but at that moment there was the sound of running feet, and his sister Ellie and Cousin Cynthia appeared, wearing a strange assortment of gaudy fake furs (which clashed horribly with Cynthia's bright orange hair and green eyes) and scarves and ridiculously high-heeled shoes. Cynthia took one look at Ben's shocked face, then at the ripped bag, and finally at the cat licking its paws. And then she started to laugh. It was the sort of laugh that brought to Ben's mind the image of someone poking a piglet with a broomstick. It was a laugh that brought Ben's mother to the door. She surveyed the scene with a single raised eyebrow.

"It sounds as if someone's having fun!"

Cynthia was laughing so hard that she fell off her shoes. Even that didn't shut her up. Tears of mirth were rolling down her cheeks, but Ben was still mystified. "Oh, cats!" squealed Cynthia. "They're so . . . cruel!"

Mrs. Arnold cast a contemptuous gaze at her niece, now sprawling on the lawn, clutching her sides. Finally her gaze came to rest on the step. "Well, well," she said. "It looks as if someone's dropped something there."

Cynthia giggled harder. "That cat . . . ," she indicated the big ginger tom, now threading its way sinuously between the palings of the gate, its tail curled over like a great big question mark. "He"—she snorted with laughter—"he's eaten Ben's new fish!"

Ben started to say something, then stopped. He stared at the wet doorstep; then at the retreating tomcat; then at the cardboard box, which offered no help at all, other than a few white whiskers that poked briefly through one of the airholes then quickly withdrew from sight.

"Oh, Ben . . . ," said Ellie, for once at a loss for words.

"All that time," said his mother. "All that effort . . ."

But Ben's head was bent, which was just as well, since a wide, secret smile had started to spread itself across his face.

His relief was not to last for long.

"And look!" cried Cousin Cynthia, picking herself up with alacrity and swooping upon the cardboard box. "What's this?"

Ben's heart fell like a stone to the bottom of his sneakers.

"Ben's bought me some food for my new pet!"


A short while later Cynthia and her father left, Uncle Aleister huffily reinserting the piranhas' tank and filtration unit into the trunk of the car, Cynthia grasping her two ill-gotten cans of Kit-e-Kat to her meager chest. There seemed to be something wrong with her face, but Ben couldn't quite work out what it was. With a loud honk and a squeal of brakes, the Jag sped off down the road in the direction of town. Ellie, Ben, and their parents watched it go in silence. Then Mr. Arnold shook his head. "I know he's your brother, Izzie, love," he said to Mrs. Arnold, "but I just can't stand the man. All he talks about is money."

"Ah, but Clive," Mrs. Arnold said, patting his arm, "I'm sure he's none the happier for it."

"Not with a daughter like Cynthia," Ben said, very quietly.

Ellie stifled a giggle.

For a moment neither of their parents said anything. Then his father laughed. "No wonder the piranhas ate each other," he said. He kissed the top of his wife's head. "I'll make us a cup of tea."

"What about you, Ben?" his mother asked gently. Her eyebrow rose again into what Mr. Arnold called her "quizzical" expression.

"I'm all right," Ben replied. "I'm just going to walk around the yard for a bit."

As his father pushed the wheelchair down the hall toward the kitchen, Ben, still puzzling over the mystery of the disappearance of the phantom fish, thought he heard his father say something about Cynthia and a cat, but he couldn't quite make it out.

## Chapter Four

# The Secret Country

As soon as they had all disappeared into the kitchen, Ben picked up the cardboard box. It came up into his hands so easily that he almost overbalanced. Something was wrong, his head told him. It was too light. . . .

It was empty.

Ben stood up and stared wildly around, but he could see neither hide nor hair of the cat. He wondered whether Cynthia had stolen it, or if it had somehow escaped from the box and wandered off. He thought about calling out for it, but then realized that he had no idea of its name. Instead, he walked around the front yard, calling "Kitty, Kitty!" but this sounded plain ridiculous; besides, within a few minutes it seemed that several other cats answered to that name, since they kept appearing stealthily: on the front wall, beside the gate, on the fence, poking their heads through the hedge. Ben looked at them crossly.

"Go away!" he said fiercely. "You're not my kitten."

A thin white cat with a sharply angled head and pale eyes slid through the gate.

"You're a very rude boy," she said, quite distinctly.

Ben stared at her. After a moment he pulled himself together and said, "So you can talk too."

The white cat laughed. So did all the others. A fat brown cat with a patch of gold over one eye waddled across the lawn and wheezed up at him, "Of course we can talk. How'd you like it if we treated you like a complete idiot? Show some respect."

Ben frowned. "Eh?"

"Hay is for horses," said the white cat primly. "Didn't your mother teach you manners? You should beg his pardon."

"Sorry," said Ben automatically. He ran a hand across his forehead, and it came away beaded with sweat. Whatever was he doing, apologizing to a group of cats? He stared around in case his father came out and saw him. (His mother would think nothing of it: She talked to things all the time, animate or inanimate—she talked to flies and spiders and plants; she talked to the car, to the vacuum, to the washing machine; once he'd even caught her lecturing a fork.) "I must be going mad," he said to himself. "Completely and utterly bats. It's probably genetic."

"In my opinion, all humans are mad." This came from the big ginger cat he had seen earlier. It was standing at full stretch up against the garden gate with its elbows on the top, a most bizarrely humanlike posture. As if to allay suspicions, it dropped at once to all fours.

"What do you mean?" Ben wondered, feeling obscurely insulted.

All the cats laughed like a pack of hyenas, as if they'd all been waiting for this.

"Humans!" proclaimed the big ginger tom. "Humans are big and slow and completely devoid of magic."

Ben decided to change the subject. "I'm looking for my kitten," he said. "It was in that box over by the door just a minute ago. Have you seen it anywhere?"

The white cat tutted. "It," she said. "It, indeed. You wouldn't think us very polite if we called you 'it,' would you?" Then she winked at him. Or perhaps she just had something in her eye. "Besides," she added, "I don't think he'd thank you for calling him a kitten!"

"I'm sorry," said Ben. "I don't know anything about him. I just bought him from Mr. Dodds's pet shop. He is a bit scrawny, though, for a grown-up cat. . . ."

A hush fell over the group. Four or five of them went into a secretive huddle and began whispering urgently. At last the group broke apart. The fat brown cat appeared to have been elected the cats' speaker, for he bushed out his tail in a rather self-important fashion, cleared his throat, and said, "No one can ever own a cat, young man, so we regret we cannot aid you in your search. It would be a grave disservice to catkind for another of our number to fall under human oppression. Too many cats have been bought and sold against their will, only to be labeled and collared in a most demeaning fashion." He indicated his own collar—a handsome affair of red velvet, complete with a silver bell and a plastic name tag.

The ginger tom leaped gracefully over the front gate and landed at Ben's feet. He stared insolently at the fat brown cat and said in a dismissive tone, "There's no need for any of this nonsense. I know exactly where the Wanderer is. Follow me."

So saying, he trotted quickly through the front garden, past the Morris and the bins, one of which was lying on its side with its contents strewn around on the paving stones, and through the alleyway into the backyard. He went unerringly across the lawn until he stood at the base of the apple tree. "He's up there," he said, indicating the tree house.

The little cat was waiting for him. He had made himself comfortable on an old blanket and was grooming nonchalantly. Ben hauled himself up through the hole in the tree house floor and regarded him wearily.

"Right, then," he said. "Tell me exactly what's going on—why did you stop me buying my fish? What does the world need saving from? And what was all that with the burst bag on the doorstep?" He stopped to draw breath. The Wanderer just smiled.

"And how come I'm suddenly plagued by talking cats? And who are you, anyway?"

"Now calm down, Ben," the cat said in a cowboy drawl. "Let's take this one step at a time, shall we? In the first place, I didn't make you do anything; you chose to rescue me—even if it was in response to my heartfelt plea—and it was extremely kind of you to give up all your savings in order to do so.

"We'll come to saving the world later, shall we? And as for the fish—well . . ." He grimaced. "They weren't exactly as advertised, as is so often the case in life, and especially in Mr. Dodds's Pet Emporium."

The Wanderer stretched out a leg and started to groom in a finicky fashion between his spread toes.

"Keep going," said Ben fiercely.

"Just being polite," said the cat. "I mean, if we're going to do proper introductions, you don't want to shake hands while I've still got the stench of that pet shop on me, do you?" He sniffed his foreleg again, gave it a final lick. "That's better. Just smells of cat spit now." Grinning evilly, he extended a paw, but Ben was not the sort of boy to be put off by a bit of saliva. Grasping the cat by the paw, he gave it a firm shake, just as his father had taught him.

The cat winced. "Ow, no need to try and break my leg."

"Sorry," said Ben. "Look, this paw-shaking is all very well, but you know my name and all I know about you is that the ginger cat called you 'the Wanderer.'"

The cat smiled proudly. "Yes, indeed. I was born into a family of great explorers. My father was Polo Horatio Coromandel, and my mother the famous Finna Sorvo Farwalker. We are well known for our expeditioning. My father climbed Cloudbeard, the highest mountain in Eidolon, the year before I was born; and my mother, well, she founded a colony in the New West before sailing on to discover the Unipeds of Whiteland. She was the one who discovered the highway that leads into your Valley of the Kings."

"Sailed?"

"With her great friend Letitia, the giant otter."

This all sounded very impressive and entirely fictional. "And what have you done to earn *your* title?" Ben asked.

The cat looked uncomfortable. "Ah, well, you know, wandered about a bit. Made some long journeys. Came here . . ."

"Obviously."

The little cat cleared his throat and changed the subject quickly. "I am going to give you a gift, because of who you are. I would not entrust my name to just anyone, for the gift of a true name carries with it a responsibility as well as power over the giver."

Ben was rather lost by this, so he said nothing.

The cat looked him steadily in the eye. "Our fortunes are bound up together," he said. "I can feel it in my marrow. Can I trust you, Ben Arnold?" He reached out and placed a paw on Ben's arm. Ben could feel the points of the claws cool and sharp against his skin. He nodded dumbly. Then something struck him. "I didn't tell you my name, so how do you know it?"

In response, the little cat tapped the side of his nose. "That's for me to know and you to find out," he said irritatingly. Then he tightened his grip on Ben's arm, the claws digging in like needles.

"Ow!"

"Now give me your full name."

Ben hesitated. If names really did give someone power over you, could he trust this strange little cat, who had already played a number of tricks on him?

He regarded the creature solemnly. The cat stared back, unblinking.

Ben made his decision.

"Benjamin Christopher Arnold."

"Benjamin Christopher Arnold, I thank you for your gift, and hereby entrust to you in exchange my own full and secret title and the power it has over me." He took a deep breath. "My name is Ignatius Sorvo Coromandel, also known as the Wanderer. But you can call me Iggy."

"Iggy?"

The little cat shrugged. "You have to admit the other's a bit of a mouthful. All cats have a short name they give freely to others. You may know a couple of the local cats as Spot and Ali. But their true names begin respectively as Spotoman and Aloysius."

Ben nodded consideringly. "Okay—Iggy," he said. "That's all very well, but you've still got a lot of explaining to do."

Iggy grinned. "Let's deal with the doorstep trick first, shall we? Then we can get on to saving the world." He tucked his cleaned toes back under his belly. "It was clear that you were about to get yourself in a right old pickle coming home without your famous Mongolian Fighting Fish, what with your loud uncle booming away about the expensive tank he'd brought for you, and all. So a swift plan was hatched."

The Wanderer's topaz eyes glinted mischievously.

"I couldn't get out of the box without making a terrible racket, since some idiot had left some heavy cans on top of it, so Aby—that big orange tomcat—went off and raided your trash cans; came back with a plastic bag, just like the ones Dodds puts his fish in. I suggested he fill it with water from the birdbath, drag it back across the grass, and give it a good going-over with his claws on the doorstep. Brilliant, eh? Certainly fooled those scary girls."

"Well, yes, you fooled us all." And then Ben's heart lifted. Not only did he not have to worry about the fish or the tank, but it also meant that his father wouldn't have to go around to King Henry Close to cut Awful Uncle Aleister's hedges!

The cat watched him closely. "Now, Ben, what I am going to tell you is very dangerous information. There are only a handful of people in this world who know; and of those, most are enemies. The very fact that you can hear me singles you out, for only those with a touch of magic in them can hear what cats say. For that reason alone, I have decided to place my trust in you. That, and the goodness of your heart. I do believe, Ben, that you have a good heart."

Ben felt himself blushing.

"Listen carefully to what I tell you, for it is a remarkable story."

Iggy shuffled around on the blanket until he had made himself fully comfortable, then he began: "There is a Secret Country, which no true human being has ever seen. It lies between here and there; between yesterday, today, and tomorrow; between the light and the dark; it lies tangled between the deepest roots of ancient trees, and yet it also soars among the stars; it is everywhere and nowhere. Its name is Eidolon, and it is my home."

This all sounded rather peculiar, and to be honest, Ben thought, a trifle excessive. But Eye-do-lon. It had a certain resonance. . . .

"It is a land of magic. . . ."

Now Ben looked disbelieving.

"Long ago," continued the Wanderer, "there was only one world. It was a wonderful place, full of extraordinary beings. Every creature you could ever imagine lived there: dogs and rabbits, cats and elephants, horses and frogs, fish and birds and insects. But there were also those that you humans think of as mythical—like the dragon and the unicorn, the gryphon and the satyr, the centaur and the banshee and the minotaur. And those you regard as 'extinct'—dinosaurs and dodos, mammoths and saber-toothed tigers and giant sloths. People lived there too, but in many different forms: giants and goblins, fairies and elves, trolls and mermaids and witches and dryads and nymphs. Then a great comet came flying through space and hit it so hard that it flew apart. And when it came back together, it was as two worlds. All the magic that had ever existed fell away into the Shadow World, the place we know as Eidolon, or the Secret Country. The world in which you live is what was left when all the magic was gone from it."

Ben laughed. "I don't believe in magic. Tricks, yes, but not real magic. I've seen those TV programs where they show you how magicians fake their illusions—all those mirrors and false floors and invisible string and stuff."

"Mummery and legerdemain have always existed," Iggy said mildly. "But that's not what I mean. You would need to come to Eidolon to see real magic at work. Here it fades to nothing more than shimmer and shine. Oh, and the ability to speak with beasts." He regarded Ben quizzically.

"What are you saying? That because I can speak to you and hear you talking to me I must have magic in me that comes from this other place?"

"From the Secret Country, Ben; yes. As I told you, it is my home. But in some part, it is also yours. I knew it as soon as you walked into the shop. You smell of Eidolon."

How rude! Ben stared at him.

"I do not. I wash every day. Well, almost."

The cat grinned at him. "I have a remarkably good nose."

## Chapter Five

# Instances of Magic

"Who are you talking to?"

Ben stuck his head down through the hole in the floor of the tree house. His sister Ellie was standing at the bottom of the apple tree, staring up at him.

At the sound of her voice, Iggy began to burrow frantically under the old blanket until he eventually disappeared from view, apart from the very tip of his tail.

Ellie started to climb the peg-ladder that led up the tree.

Ben flicked the blanket over the twitching tail and then flung himself down next to it, carefully masking the bulge of the Wanderer with an opened comic.

"Er, no one."

"Talking to yourself is considered mad in most civilized circles, you know."

Ellie's head appeared, truncated at the neck by the tree house's decking. She was four years older than her brother, and those years made a world of difference. All she was interested in, it seemed to Ben, was fashion. Her room was scattered with magazines and scraps of fabric, the walls invisible beneath a papering of sullen models in bizarre garments, and about a million mirrors, in which she checked her face and hair every three seconds. (In contrast, Ben's room contained piles of books and comics and a jumble of objects: a piece of flint that looked just like a dragon's claw, fossils and star charts, unusually shaped bits of wood. There was a mirror in there somewhere, but Ben never used it.) Ellie's room smelled of perfumes and powders, lotions and nail polish. Today, it seemed, Ellie and

Cynthia had been experimenting with makeup, for his sister's eyes had acquired a startling and unsettling definition. (Which would explain why Awful Cousin Cynthia had looked even more awful than usual.) Unfortunately, whatever effect Ellie had been trying to achieve was rather spoiled by a long smear of mascara beneath one lower lid, which had given her a slightly lopsided look, as if her face wasn't entirely in control of itself, and by the hideous shade of purple glitter-shadow she had applied to the upper lids.

"Gross!" said Ben. "You look as if someone's smacked you in both eyes!"

Ellie curled her lip at him. It was smudged a livid and slippery pink. So were her teeth. "It's Dior," she snarled, as if this explained everything. "You wouldn't understand."

"Anyway," said Ben, "what do you want?"

"It's time for tea. Mum and Dad have been calling you for ages."

"I'm not hungry."

"No?" Ellie raised a badly penciled eyebrow. "It's shepherd's pie. And Mum's melted cheese on top."

"I'll be down in a minute, okay?"

"Why, what are you trying to hide from me?"

With an arm swifter than a striking snake, she snatched the comic out of his hands.

"It's a graphic novel," Ben said. He maneuvered himself squarely between her and the lump now revealed in the blanket. "*The Sandman*. It's about Morpheus, the Lord of Dreams, who rules over the world we enter when we sleep. It's famous. It's won awards."

"Another world? Really?" Ellie riffled through it. She stopped at one page, turned it sideways, and scrutinized the illustration. For a moment, curiosity softened the mask of superiority she usually adopted. Then she tucked it under her arm. "Right, I'm confiscating this!"

And before he could say anything, she swung herself back down the peg-ladder and ran toward the house. Ben watched her go and felt no irritation, no anger; nothing but relief. He lifted a corner of the blanket.

The cat's nose quested out and sniffed the air once, twice, three times. Then his head emerged.

"It's all right, Iggy, she's gone."

"So that's your sister, is it, Ben?"

Ben nodded. "Ellie, yes. Eleanor."

"Eleanor Arnold."

"Eleanor Katherine Arnold," Ben said suddenly, then clapped his hands over his mouth. What had he given away?

"Eleanor Katherine Arnold," the Wanderer said softly, as if committing this to memory. "Ah, yes."

"I have to go now," said Ben. He reached out to the little cat but Iggy flinched away.

"You should never touch a cat—or indeed any creature—unless invited," Iggy said sternly. "Humans can be so ill-mannered."

"I'm sorry," said Ben. He seemed to be spending his whole day apologizing to cats. "Can we talk about saving the world later?"

"You'll have to bring me something to eat," Iggy said pragmatically. "Otherwise I'll have to raid a trash can or two. It can make a bit of a mess, and I wouldn't want you to get into any more trouble."

"That's blackmail!" Ben thought regretfully of the two tins of catfood Cousin Cynthia had swiped. Heaven knew what else he could find.

Ignatius Sorvo Coromandel shrugged. "That's life." His eyes glowed enigmatically.

* * *

By the time he got inside, though, Ben could hardly eat, he was so excited by the day's strange events. Luckily, no one was paying much attention to him, since Ellie was getting lectured on the overuse of cosmetics. "It's just not attractive, darling, plastering yourself like that," his mother was saying. "Besides, I thought the natural look was in."

"This *is* the natural look," Ellie said sulkily. "I could have put loads more on if I'd wanted to. Cynthia did."

"Natural, if you want that 'I've-just-gone-ten-rounds-with-Mike-Tyson' sort of look, I suppose," Mr. Arnold muttered.

Ellie flung down her cutlery. "Honestly, it's like living in the Middle Ages round here—you have no idea!" Sighing theatrically, she flounced off to the sofa and switched on the television.

The six o'clock news had just started. A woman in a buttoned-up blouse and a sensible jacket was looking seriously out of the set and explaining to viewers that main street shops were reporting a slight rise in their earnings this month.

"That'll be a result of all the money Eleanor's spending on eyeshadow," Mr. Arnold said very softly to Ben, making sure that Ellie didn't hear. Ben smiled. Since the doorstep incident, his parents were being extra kind to him, he noticed: His father had given him the largest helping of shepherd's pie, with the crispiest cheese, and his mother had yet to suggest he tidy his room, his usual Saturday chore. And no one had mentioned the Mongolian Fighting Fish at all.

"And finally," came the voice on the television, "the Test Match at Lords was interrupted this after-noon by a rather unusual pitch invasion."

Ben craned his neck. The screen showed a wide expanse of brilliant green field, dotted with white-clad cricketers. Instead of concentrating on the play, they were all staring at the far end of the ground, where there was a bit of a commotion. A lot of people were running around with their arms outstretched, as if try-ing to catch something. The camera zoomed in for a close-up. It appeared that a small white horse had somehow gotten on to the pitch and was now in a panic because of all the attention it was receiving. It reared up, and for a moment Ben could have sworn that it had a tall, spiraling horn attached to its fore-head; then it bucked and darted for the edge of the field and disappeared into the crowd. Spectators scrambled out of its way, and a few seconds later it was gone.

Mrs. Arnold watched it, her green eyes wide with what might have been amazement, or shock. "Oh," she said, her hands pressed against cheeks that had gone ivory white. "Oh, no . . ."

"Typical," said Mr. Arnold. "It's the only way England can get a draw. Unicorn stops play. Whatever next?"

"It *was* a unicorn, wasn't it, Dad?" Ben asked earnestly.

Mr. Arnold grinned. "Of course it was, son."

From the sofa came a great howl of derision from his sister. "Don't be stupid! Of course it wasn't a unicorn—they don't exist. It was just some poor sad little pony someone had tied a whopping great horn on for a joke."

"They do exist!" Ben said crossly. "In . . ."—he hesitated—"another world."

Mrs. Arnold stared at her son, her eyes sparking green fire. She opened her mouth as if to say something, then closed it again.

Ellie laughed. She held up the graphic novel she'd taken from him and waved it around. "You'd better tell him to stop filling his head with this garbage. He'll rot his brain."

Ben charged from his chair and hurled himself over the sofa on top of his sister. After a lot of scuffling and hair-pulling, he emerged triumphantly with *The Sandman*, now rather bent and battered, tucked under his arm. From the other side of the room, a terrible high-pitched wail broke out.

"Now you've woken Alice!" his mother cried. She looked pale and drawn, as if she might faint at any moment. Tears sparkled in her eyes and at once Ben felt terribly guilty.

"Sorry, Mum," he gulped, hanging his head. When he looked up again, hoping she would give him her usual smile, he found she wasn't looking at him but was staring at the television as if it had in some way betrayed her.

Mr. Arnold intervened. "I won't have you two fighting like cat and dog! See how you've upset your mother. You can both take the rest of your dinner and go up to your rooms. I don't want to see you down here again before breakfast."

Even though he wasn't feeling hungry any longer, Ben grabbed his plate and a fork from the table and went slowly up the stairs. When he reached the land-ing, he gazed out of the tall, arched window that over-looked the backyard. The tree house showed no sign of its new occupant. Nothing stirred, except for a big blue dragonfly lazily quartering the air above the lawn, hunting down unwary insects. Ben watched it for a while, entranced by its graceful aerobatics and by the way the rays of the setting sun made its body shimmer and shine; then he opened the door to his room and shut it carefully behind him.

The window in Ben's room opened on to the alley at the side of the house. It was also conveniently close to the large black drainpipe that ran from the bath-room down the brick wall to the ground. Ben gave the drainpipe a good, hard stare. A few minutes later he heard Ellie's door slam shut and the latest Blue Flamingos album come on. Alice had stopped crying, and the only noise coming from downstairs now was a comfortable hum of conversation and canned laughter from some television sitcom.

For the next hour Ben forced himself to concentrate on his math homework.

The sun went down and the moon rose to take its place amongst the clouds. A dog howled and a car pulled out of a driveway farther down the street. Inside the house all was quiet.

Ben slid the remains of the shepherd's pie into the only container he could find in his room—a baseball cap advertising the local newspaper for which his father worked (*The Bixbury Gazette*)—and lowered it out of the window on a length of string. Then he swung his legs out over the sill and transferred his weight gingerly onto the drainpipe, gripping the slick plastic tube tight between his knees. His heart hammered with the anticipation of an adventure about to begin. The drainpipe creaked and the metal brackets holding it to the brickwork rattled, but it seemed secure.

Ben hated games at school. He was hopeless at rugby (all those people kicking you), didn't like swimming (cold, wet, and no matter what he did, he always sank to the bottom like a stone), and as for gym, how tedious was it to go up rope after rope, or jump endlessly over tattered leather "horses"? But curiously enough, all those hours of rope-climbing seemed to have paid off. He jammed his sneakers into the space between the drainpipe and the wall and, shifting his balance carefully, worked his way down hand over hand, in excellent style.

At the bottom, he retrieved the baseball cap and its

gooey contents and ran silently down the passage. The poor cat must be starving by now. Did cats eat shepherd's pie, he wondered, and if so, would they eat a congealed one with cheese on top? Had Ignatius been a dog, he would have had no qualms at all, for dogs seemed to eat anything, including things no right-minded creature would touch, but he wasn't too sure about cats.

At the end of the alley, he came out into the backyard. Pale moonlight silvered the grass and filtered through the apple tree to send shadows stretching toward him like long, spiky fingers.

Even in the wan light, he could see there was something lying in the middle of the lawn. From where he stood, it looked shiny and metallic, a bit like a crumpled chip packet. He glanced back at the house to make sure no one was watching him, then crept quietly across the grass. When he reached the middle of the lawn, he looked down. Whatever it was, it was certainly not a chip packet, that much was clear. He knelt to examine it closer. Four great glistening wings were curled over a long, still, iridescent body. He felt a moment of pure sadness when he remembered how magnificently the dragonfly had swooped and cruised around the garden. Clearly it would never fly again. He touched it with a finger. Perhaps it was asleep. Did dragonflies sleep? The middle of someone's lawn was probably not the best spot to choose, he thought, especially with a hungry cat only a few yards away up a tree.

As if in response to the gentle pressure of his finger, the dragonfly stirred briefly. One of the gauzy wings fell a little to one side, and suddenly Ben found himself staring down at the most extraordinary thing he had ever seen.

It was not a dragonfly at all.

It was a fairy.

## Chapter Six

# Twig

Ben could hardly believe his eyes. Whatever was happening in the world? Or should he say, *this* world? A unicorn on the television news, a talking cat up in the tree house, and now a fairy on his very own lawn . . .

He picked it up gently. It was lighter than he expected, and dry-feeling, like a dead leaf. He hardly dared close his hand on it; it seemed so fragile, for all its size. Already the iridescence on its body and wings was fading, just as the scales of a freshly caught fish quickly lose that glossy sheen that made you want to catch it in the first place. Cradling the fairy in one arm, he approached the tree house. He put the base-ball cap on the ground at the foot of the apple tree, wrapped the string attached to it around his hand, and climbed up the peg-ladder, being careful not to bump the fairy on the way.

It was very dark inside the tree house; so dark, in fact, that he did not see Ignatius Sorvo Coromandel until he trod on his tail. The dozing cat yowled so loudly that Ben, in fright, almost dropped the fairy. He juggled it desperately, caught it by a wing, and scooped it back into his arms. Iggy, disorientated and furious, his hackles sticking out like the ruff of a frilled lizard, was dancing high on his toes, tail bushed out to the size of a feather duster. Moonlight reflected from eyes that looked mad for battle. At that moment, he did not much resemble Ben's fond ideas of what a fluffy pet cat should be.

"I'm really sorry," said Ben. "I didn't see you."

"Again the boy apologizes," Iggy sighed. "Humans," he muttered darkly. "They're all the same. Completely useless."

"I'm not useless," Ben said huffily. "I've brought you two things you'll be very interested in."

The cat's eyes gleamed.

"Food?" he asked hopefully.

"That might be one of them," Ben conceded. "But first, look at this. I found it on the lawn."

He knelt and laid the fairy carefully at Iggy's feet. The cat took a swift step backward. "By the Lady! A wood-sprite. Where did you say you found it?"

Ben pointed down through the hole. "Over there. I saw it flying around earlier on, but I thought it was a dragonfly."

Iggy sniffed at the wood-sprite. "Still alive, though barely." He opened his jaws wide and shoveled at the creature's body. After angling his head awkwardly several times, he said, "He's quite big, isn't he? For a wood-sprite."

In the darkness, Ben grimaced. "I don't know. How big do they get?"

The little cat sat back on his haunches. "Oh, some are so long. . . ." He stretched his front paws out wide. "But most are about this size. . . ." He brought them closer together. "But you should see some of the goblins in Darkmere Forest. . . ." He whistled through his teeth. "You don't want to meet one of those on a dark night."

His stomach rumbled so loudly that it reverberated off the walls of the tree house. "Whoops, sorry. Better attend to this little fellow, then you can show me what else you've brought for me. I'm so hungry, I could eat my own tail."

Ben picked the wood-sprite up and carried it across to the blanket, where Ignatius crouched over it, his back to the boy. In the gloom, Ben could not quite see what the cat was doing; but after a while he heard the wet, clicking sound of a mouth hard at work, and for a terrible moment he thought Iggy's hunger had got the better of him and that he was eating the fairy. He must have made a noise, for Iggy's head came up sharply. The cat licked his lips. "Cat-spit mends all," he said. "According to my mother . . ."

Ben eyed the cat skeptically. "You can't just lick someone back to life."

But against all the odds, the wood-sprite was stirring. Dopily, it raised itself onto one thin elbow. It rubbed its face with a spidery hand and its eyes came open. Even in the dark, Ben could see that its eyes were remarkable: prismatic, many-colored, as round as Christmas baubles. It said something in a tinny, scratchy voice, then sank down again, exhausted.

"His name is . . ." Iggy made a sound rather like the creaking of a branch. "You'd better call him Twig. He says he is dying."

"What's the matter with him?"

"He's dying of being here."

"Why?"

"There isn't enough magic here to sustain him. A wood-sprite is a creature that can live only in the element for which it is adapted, and that's the woodland of the Secret Country."

"But how did he get here?"

"I wish I knew. The only way in and out of Eidolon is by way of the wild roads—"

"What?"

Iggy sighed. "Questions, all the time, questions." He rubbed his face wearily. "I will tell you what—feed me and then I'll try to explain. You probably won't understand it all, but that's because you're largely human—"

Ben started to complain, but Ignatius held up a peremptory paw, then pointed to his open mouth. "Food first, sonny."

Gritting his teeth, Ben hauled up the baseball cap. It seemed heavier than before, and when he got it over the lip of the entrance, he understood why. It was full of slugs. "Ugh!"

"Well," said Ignatius reasonably, "whatever do you expect, leaving such a feast lying around unattended like that?" He bent his head to the cap and sniffed. "Smells good. No, I take that back: It smells wonderful!"

Ben wrinkled his nose in disgust. He'd always thought cats were such fastidious animals, the way they groomed and fussed over themselves. Now he was beginning to have his doubts.

Ignatius was whispering to the cap. After a few moments, the slugs started to wave their antennae at one another as if in debate, then one by one they slithered up out of the baseball cap and trundled off down the tree. The paths they had made to the exit glittered, all silver slime in the moonlight.

"What did you say to them?"

"I told them you'd eat them if they stayed."

Ben looked appalled. "Me? Eat a slug?"

"I'd heard that humans ate all manner of peculiar things," Iggy said indistinctly, through a mouthful of cold shepherd's pie. "I'm sure I heard somewhere of people eating slugs."

"That's snails, and I'm not French," Ben said shortly.

"Ah, well," said Iggy, sounding a lot more cheerful, "did the trick, though, didn't it? Not very bright, slugs, get a bit confused sometimes. They rather aspire to being snails, having their own houses, and all." He ate in relative silence for a while, his head disappearing farther and farther into the baseball cap. Surely he wasn't going to eat the lot? But then there came the clear sound of the rasp of tongue against fabric, and Ignatius Sorvo Coromandel emerged with a deeply satisfied expression on his face. His belly bulged as if he had swallowed a rubber ball whole.

"Now then, where were we?"

"Wild roads," Ben reminded him.

"Ah, yes. The magic highways. Cats are by nature curious creatures, and also great explorers; so when the worlds separated, it was cats who nosed around and found that there were places where the worlds touched, and that if you had a good enough nose, you could find a way through from one to the other, and even back again. If enough cats followed the same path, back and forth, a wild road was made. We cats like to have the best of both worlds, you know." He grinned at his feeble joke. When he realized Ben wasn't smiling, he went on with a more authoritative tone, "The trouble is, there are others who can use the wild roads, others who can exist in both worlds. But they must own a dual nature, for if they do not, they sicken and die."

"What do you mean?" asked Ben, frowning, "by a dual nature?"

Iggy regarded him with his head on one side. He looked from Ben's green eye to his brown eye and back again and became thoughtful. After a moment he said, "Some creatures, like cats, are both wild *and* tame, both magical and mortal, though a pet cat may seem more tame than wild to you as it cries for its tinned food and rolls on its back in play. But don't be deceived: In even the soppiest of pets lies the wildest of hunters and explorers. We live by day and by night; we can see by sun or by starlight; we can be visible to the human eye one moment, the next we're . . ."

The word "gone" hung for a moment in the night air, then there was a sudden scuffle of movement that had Ben spinning around for the source of the noise.

When he turned back, Iggy had vanished. Just like that. And here he was, all on his own with a dying fairy. Typical.

"Where are you?" he called crossly.

There was no reply. Ben's eyes strained against the thick darkness, but it was impossible to see anything. To make sure he did not accidentally tread on Twig as he had on the cat's tail, he picked him up, cupping him gently in both hands. The wood-sprite's eyes flickered at Ben's touch, and then, as if by magic, an eerie blue-green light pulsed out of his body. It illuminated every nook and cranny of the tree house, but there was no sign of Ignatius at all.

"All right, Iggy, very clever. Now come back!"

Silence.

Then: "Cat . . . up . . . there . . ." The words were quite unmistakable. Ben stared at the wood-sprite in amazement.

"What did you say?"

Twig sighed, a small sound like a breeze through leaves. Feebly he pointed above Ben's head, but before Ben could say anything, a bizarre croaking sound split the night. Ben stared up, and Ignatius Sorvo Coromandel was revealed, bathed in Twig's uncanny light, hanging by his claws from the ceiling. He dropped neatly to Ben's feet and burped.

"Oops, sorry! Still, better out than in."

"That was just a trick, and not a very good one. I can't see what it's got to do with wild roads at all."

Iggy shook his head. "I knew you wouldn't understand," he said. A hiccup escaped him, racking his whole body. Then another, and another. Ben stood there with the wood-sprite in his hands, regarding the cat unsympathetically.

Twig's eyes flickered, and the green light began to fade. Ben lifted him up and blew warm air onto his face, but the little creature only stirred weakly, twisting away from him, then lay still once more. "Iggy, he's dying again!" he cried in panic. He laid the wood-sprite down on the floor in front of the cat, who scrutinized him closely.

"It's better that you don't touch him too often," the cat said gently. His hiccups appeared to have subsided. "You probably squeezed him a bit hard when you picked him up. Wood-sprites tend to shine like that when they feel under threat, but it uses up their strength."

"But I wouldn't hurt him for the world—," Ben started miserably.

"This world—and everything in it—is a threat to him, as it is to all the creatures of the Secret Country. And that's the problem we have to fix."

Another scratchy sound. "Tell boy didn't hurt . . . dozing . . . pick me up . . . panic."

Ben was silent for a moment. Then he knelt beside the sprite. "I'm really sorry, Twig," he said.

Twig made a grimace that might have been a smile, showing two long rows of tiny teeth that shone as sharp as needles and looked as if they could give you a nasty nip. Then he closed his eyes. "Sleep . . . now," he said indistinctly.

Ben turned to the cat. "Is that true of unicorns?"

"Eh?"

"Hay is for horses," Ben corrected sternly, remembering the little white cat. "Though I suppose unicorns might eat hay too."

Iggy frowned. "Unicorns?"

*That got him*, Ben thought, with grim satisfaction. "If this world is a threat to all the creatures of the Secret Country, then how come the unicorn I saw on TV this afternoon looked just fine?" he asked. "There it was, kicking up its heels, interrupting the cricket."

"Cricket?"

"It's a game with two teams of eleven players, though they're not all on the pitch at the same time . . . in fact, there are only ever thirteen players on at once—unless one of the batsmen's using a runner; though I suppose technically both of them might be, which would make fifteen; oh, and the umpire, of course. He's the one covered in sweaters. And they use bats to hit a ball around a big field."

Iggy looked horrified. In his confusion he saw a crowd of crickets and grasshoppers cornering a victim, the so-called umpire, and leaping up and down on its body. And those poor bats . . . What a terrible place this world was. He shivered. "I hesitate to ask, but how does the unicorn come into this?"

Ben explained what he'd seen.

"A unicorn, here . . ." A fearful light shone in the little cat's eyes. "Someone is up to no good; and I know who!" He clutched Ben by the arm. "We must leave at once."

Ben drew back. "We?"

"Someone must carry the wood-sprite."

"And go where?"

"Why, to Eidolon, of course."

"To the Secret Country?"

"At once."

"For how long?"

Iggy shrugged. "A few days? A week? A month?"

"But I've got school on Monday!"

Iggy's claws tightened on his arm. "The natural balance of two worlds is under threat, Ben, and you worry about school?"

An unreadable expression crossed Ben's face. Then he grinned.

"Great!" he said. "I'll miss swimming!"

## Chapter Seven

# Something Fishy

If he was going to the Secret Country, Ben thought, he'd better leave a note, or his parents would go postal.

He rummaged around in his treasure chest (an old wooden box he used as a seat) and emerged eventually (after casting aside a one-armed Gollum, a Dalek with no antenna, and a headless Incredible Hulk; a dozen tattered comics; a much-thumbed copy of *The*

*Hobbit*, a half-eaten Mars bar, and some poster paints) with a spiralbound notebook, a chewed pen, and (triumphantly) a pound coin. First of all he wrote:

Dear Mum and Dad,
   Ellie is in league with Cousin Cynthia. If I stay she will sell me to her as pet food for whatever monster she owns now, so I have run away to sea.
   Love,
   Ben

He crossed it out; knowing his mother, she'd think it was true.

He started again.

Dear Mum and Dad,
   I met a talking cat and a dying fairy who come from another world called the Secret Country. I have to help them find their way back, or Twig will die.
   Remember that unicorn? It was real! See you soon.
   Lots of love,
   Ben

Then he tore that up too—you never knew who might find it, and it was giving away a lot of important information.

After several more attempts (it was hard to write when you couldn't see what you were doing and the cat would not allow you to use the wood-sprite even for a moment's illumination) Ben wrote:

Dear Mum and Dad,
    Please don't worry about me. I'll be back soon. It's a matter of life and death! (Not mine, I hope.)
    Lots of love,
    Ben

He left the note on the front doorstep with a stone on top to prevent it from blowing away. Carrying Twig in the roughly cleaned baseball cap, and with his notebook and pen in his pocket, he followed Ignatius Sorvo Coromandel out of the garden, tiptoed up the path, opened the creaky gate, and closed it behind him as quietly as he could. Out on Underhill Road the streetlamps bathed everything in an eerie orange glow, so that the whitewashed houses looked as if they'd been drenched in stale Tang.

"Right, then." He looked at Iggy expectantly. "Where's this wild road?"

The cat shrugged. "I don't know."

"You don't know?"

"It's not that simple. They're a bit of a maze. You have to get the right one to start off with, or you could end up anywhere. You could get well and truly lost— find yourself in Outer Mongolia in 1207." He shuddered.

Ben thought hard for a moment. "Genghis Khan— brilliant!" His eyes gleamed. "The Golden Horde, sweeping down through the Asian steppes, killing everyone in their path. Wow! I'd love to see that."

Iggy regarded him dubiously. "You're a very bloodthirsty young man. That's why you fell for the so-called Mongolian Fighting Fish, is it? Reminded you of all those blood-and-guts tales of the Great Khan, did they?"

Ben's face fell. "Sort of."

"Well, I can tell you, sonny, that he was not a very nice man. He smelled like a yak and"—he leaned toward Ben, grinning like a demon—"he turned out to be terrified of cats!"

"I don't believe you," Ben said stiffly. "You're making this up."

"Believe what you like," Iggy said crossly. "I was there and I saw him climb up his tentpole. Now then," he said briskly. "My best suggestion is that we start with Mr. Dodds's Pet Emporium, since that's the first place I remember when I woke up in this terrible place."

It was exciting to be out on the deserted streets of Bixbury, which seemed at this still hour rather like a secret country itself. Exciting too, though he tried not to show it, to be caught up in Ignatius Sorvo Coromandel's adventure. Iggy explained as they went what had happened to him. While exploring on the edges of Eidolon's northern continent, searching, he explained, for the legendary three-tailed mouse (which no one had seen for a while) he had stumbled upon an unusual wild road. He knew as soon as he stuck his head in that it was unusual: The winds inside it all blew in the wrong direction, carrying with them bizarre aromas, aromas not familiar to an inhabitant of the Secret Country. And so he had followed his nose, driven by the curiosity of his species, and had eventually emerged here in Bixbury, of all places. But no sooner had he arrived in this world than someone had clubbed him over the head. When he woke up, he found himself in a cage, and shortly after that, Mr. Dodds had put him on sale. He showed Ben the lump on his head, just below his left ear.

"I didn't see who did it, but if I smell them again they'll be sorry." He flexed his claws. "I gave Mr. Dodds a nasty bite anyway, just to be on the safe side," he added cheerfully. He thought about that for a moment, his face suddenly queasy. "Though I wish I hadn't. He tasted simply awful."

On Quinx Lane, the Pet Emporium was dark and silent, as if everything in it—the birds and hamsters, fish and gerbils—had all been turned off along with the lights. Ben pressed his nose to the window and watched his breath flower and fade on the cold glass.

"What now?" he asked.

"We go in."

"But the door's locked," Ben said, giving it a push.

Iggy showed his teeth in what might have been a grin. "Cats can get in anywhere." So saying, he bunched his legs beneath him and leaped fluidly up onto the canopy above the shop's signboard. Another jump took him onto the upstairs window ledge, and from there he disappeared through an open fanlight. Ben had to admit he was impressed.

A minute or so later there came a rattling sound from overhead, and one of the windows came open. Ben stepped smartly into the shadows in case it was an annoyed tenant who'd had their sleep disturbed.

"Pssst! Ben!"

It was Iggy. He had no idea cats could be so dexterous.

"Come on," the Wanderer said.

"What, me, climb up there?"

The cat nodded vigorously. "Quickly now, before anyone sees you."

Ben gulped. "What about Twig?"

"Put him down whatever you call that thing you're wearing."

"My sweater?"

"Yes, yes. Now get on with it."

"But I might fall and squash him."

"We'll just have to take that chance, sonny."

"The name's Ben," Ben said crossly.

He wrapped the baseball cap closely around Twig

and slipped him down inside his sweater, which he tucked securely into his jeans. Then he examined the exterior of the pet shop. There was, of course, a drainpipe running down one side of the building. Looking up and down the street to make sure there were no witnesses to this blatant example of breaking and entering, Ben took a firm hold on the drainpipe and, wedging his feet solidly on either side, went up hand over hand till he reached the window ledge. He made the tricky transition from the pipe to the sill with his heart in his throat, and stepped cautiously through the open window.

Inside, there were a load of boxes stacked one on top of the other. Most were of the cardboard variety and had brand names of pet food stamped upon them: ToothyDog Chews; Gourmet Fishlips, Eyelids, and Earholes; Tweetiepie's Cuttlefish Heads; Stegosaur Steaks; but some were more substantial and, even to Ben's nose, smelled strange. Ignatius was poking around at the back of the room, only the tip of his twitching tail visible between the boxes.

"What are you doing?" Ben whispered. He wanted to get out of there before someone caught them.

Iggy's eyes were brilliant in the moonlight. "Look!"

Ben clambered over obstacle after obstacle to reach him.

"This is the cage they put me in. . . ." He indicated a small metal container with a hinged, slatted door. A tuft of tortoiseshell fur was still trapped in the hinge. He sniffed sadly about the cage. "I can smell the Secret Country on it," he said. "I can smell my home."

For a moment he looked so forlorn that Ben actually wanted to hug him, but Iggy came over brisk and purposeful.

"Come on," he said. "Let's see what we can find downstairs."

Ben followed him to the door and was about to open it when he trod on something hard and flat. He bent to pick it up, and his fingers had just closed on it when he heard a noise downstairs. At once Iggy became as still as only a terrified cat can be. The noise grew louder, then resolved itself into the creak of a door opening and the sound of voices. Ben shuddered.

It was Mr. Dodds.

"Hide," Iggy hissed urgently.

"Where?" Ben stared desperately about the stockroom. The boxes were too small for him to crawl into, but in the farthest corner they had been stacked up to make two tottering piles that he might just crouch behind. . . .

Footsteps on the stairs.

Iggy leaped into the cage in which he had been captured and huddled up into a ball, his eyes gleaming balefully. Ben tiptoed toward the corner, wincing at every creak and scuff his feet made on the dusty boards. The voices got closer. There was a lot of huffing and puffing, as if whoever was coming up was carrying something particularly heavy and cumbersome. Someone said, "No, you go backward," which was followed by stumbling feet, and then the door handle began to turn. . . .

Ben ran for the cover of the boxes, heart beating like a bird trapped behind his ribs. Silently, he cursed Iggy for getting him into this situation; then, rather more fairly, cursed himself for being so stupid as to follow a cat. At that moment Twig started to wriggle under his sweater. *Poor thing*, Ben thought. *He probably can't breathe down there*. He eased the sprite toward the V-neck so that it could get some air, but as soon as he did so, Twig started to glow—an eerie green that sparked like a warning beacon. It illuminated Ben's face and the expression of pure panic upon it. "No, Twig, no!" he whispered, pushing the wood-sprite back down into the depths of the sweater. "Not here!"

He stared at the two figures making their way awkwardly through the opened door. The one facing him was Mr. Dodds, no longer in his Italian suit; but he couldn't quite make out who the other man was, since he had his back to him. Luckily they were both too preoccupied with whatever they were carrying to have noticed the wood-sprite's glow. He looked down. Twig was still giving off a faint radiance, a pale green light that pulsed between the fibers of his sweater. Frantically, Ben undid some buttons on his shirt and shoved the poor wood-sprite under that as well. Twig's glow was now so feeble as to be invisible.

"Put it down there," said Mr. Dodds. "I'll ship it out in the morning."

There was more shuffling of feet as the two figures maneuvered.

"Do you think we should give it more water?" It was the other figure who spoke, but its voice sounded muffled.

"I'm exhausted. It'll survive till morning," Mr. Dodds said callously.

There was a thump as the crate they had been carrying hit the floor, then Twig sneezed.

"What was that?"

Ben held his breath. He clutched at the woodsprite in case it sneezed again. Pale green light oozed past his fingers.

Mr. Dodds strode to the light switch and flicked it on. Nothing happened.

"Darn bulb's gone!" He reached into a pocket of his overalls, took out a flashlight, and shone it negligently around the room. Ben thought his lungs might explode. His blood thundered in his head. Surely they could hear him? But Mr. Dodds tutted, clicked the flashlight off, and stuffed it back in his pocket. "You're getting paranoid. Time to go." He gave the box a kick. "We'll be back for you tomorrow," he promised.

Out they went then onto the landing. The door closed, and the sounds of footsteps and voices receded. Ben began to breathe again. He reached under his clothing and brought the wood-sprite out. It lay in his hand, its chest shuddering feebly up and down, its eyes squeezed shut as if in pain.

"Oh, Twig, I'm sorry. . . ."

At this, the sprite's eyes came open. All the color

had gone out of them in fear. It stared about blearily, then focused on Ben. "Gone?" it asked.

Ben nodded. The wood-sprite struggled to sit up. It blinked, and the last of the green light went out of it. "Know . . . them," it said. "Hurt . . . me." Then it lay back down with its arms wrapped around itself.

"Help!"

Ben jumped, startled. The noise came again, louder this time.

"HELP MEEEE-OWWWW!"

It was Iggy. Ben put Twig back inside his sweater and crossed the stockroom. He stared down at the cage. "What's the matter?"

Ignatius Sorvo Coromandel stared up at him sheepishly through the slatted metal. "I'm, er, stuck."

"How can you be stuck? You put yourself in there."

"How would I know the door had a spring on it?"

Ben shook his head. If this was the level of expertise possessed by their expedition leader, they were in a lot of trouble. He knelt down and fiddled with the catch on the cage door. It wouldn't budge.

"Oh, Iggy . . ."

"What is it?" The cat's voice held a rising note of panic.

"It, well, it seems to be locked."

"Locked?" A shriek this time. "How can it be locked? Do you think I reached out through the door and locked myself in with some invisible key? Do you think I like being in a cage? Do you think I've got some sort of imprisonment fetish?"

Ben rattled the door again, but there was no question about it: The cage was locked, and Iggy was trapped inside it. "Look," he started in the most reasonable tone he could muster, "there must be a key somewhere. I'll go downstairs and see if I can find it—"

"Don't leave me here!"

Ben wiped a hand across his forehead. Then he tried to pick up the cage, managed to move it a few inches, but the effort was too much and he dropped it rather less gently than he'd meant to.

A howl of protest came from the trapped cat.

"I'm sorry, I'm sorry. It's just really, really heavy."

"And you think that's *my* fault, do you?"

Ben didn't, but he said, "Well, you did eat all that shepherd's pie. . . ."

Iggy began to wail.

"Sssh. Please. Just for a minute or two. I'll leave you Twig for company." He laid the wood-sprite in his baseball cap on top of the cage and went swiftly out of the door before Iggy could say another word.

The pet shop was dark, but Ben didn't dare try any of the lights. He felt his way around the hall downstairs until he came to what seemed to be the office. Inside, a wash of moonlight illuminated a desk piled with paper, two wooden chairs, and a couple of old metal filing cabinets. Ben went to the desk, thinking that Mr. Dodds might keep keys in one of the drawers.

He was just about to open one when his eye was drawn by a letter lying on the desk. It had a very smart letterhead with a sort of a crest in dark ink running along the top of it.

*Dear Mr. Dodds,* he read.

*Many thanks for delivering the merchandise as requested. However, I have to say that it is not in the sort of condition I would expect, given the large sum of money I have paid you for it. Indeed, a number of its scales have already fallen off and the rest are looking decidedly unhealthy. In addition, it mopes about all day and doesn't appear to have the strength even to burn newspaper. Quite what use it is going to be as (and I quote your recent advertisement in* More Money Than Sense *magazine) "a superbly ecological garden incinerator" I can't imagine.*

*I would be grateful if you would remove the item and refund my £1,500 at once. Otherwise I may be forced to call in the Trades Descriptions people.*

*I shall look forward to hearing from you by return post.*

*Yours,*

*Lady Hawley-Fawley of Crawley*

Ben stared at the letter. One thousand five hundred pounds? What on earth could possibly cost one thousand five hundred pounds? Maybe an elephant, he reflected. But elephants didn't have scales. Or did they? And how could any animal possibly be a "garden incinerator"? Who would want to burn their garden, anyway? He couldn't imagine what it all meant. He was now beginning to feel so tired and confused by events that he couldn't think straight.

There were a lot of keys in the desk drawer. Just to make sure, Ben took them all. The fifth one he tried opened the cage, and the little cat flew out, fur bristling. Ben stroked him until he calmed down enough to start purring.

"I've been thinking," said Iggy at last. "Twig might be able to help us. Wood-sprites have an amazing sense of smell, and if they smell something they love, they glow pink all over. So when we find a wild road, we can make sure it's the right one with Twig! If you were to hold him out in front of you, he'll start to glow if we've found the one that leads to his home. At least then we'll be back in the right time zone."

"What, like divining for water?" Ben remembered seeing some people on TV once holding hazel twigs in their hands, twigs that jumped and twitched when they passed over water. Perhaps it was something twigs did.

Iggy looked at him as if he was mad. "I haven't the faintest idea what you're talking about," he said.

"Water . . ."

It was a faint voice, high and thready. Ben turned around and stared into the gloom.

"Water . . ." the voice came again. Ben could have sworn it came from the container Mr. Dodds and his accomplice had brought up to the stockroom. He and Iggy went over to it. It was a big box, about five feet long and almost two high. Rather like a small coffin. Ben tapped on it.

"Hello?" he called. "Is there someone in there?"

In response, the box began to rock and creak. Ben and Iggy leaped backward. The cat's nose started to twitch frantically. "Whoever it is comes from Eidolon," he said.

"I need water!"

Whatever it was, it sounded very demanding. "If we let you out," Ben said carefully, "will you promise not to hurt us?"

"Did you put me in here?"

"No."

"Then I won't hurt you."

Which seemed fair enough. Ben took a close look at the lock, then sorted through the pile of keys. This time, the second one he chose worked. He was getting good at this. As soon as the lock clicked, the lid of the box sprang open.

Inside was something large and mottled and sleek. It had huge, wet, dark eyes and flippers. It was a seal. In a sea green dress.

At the sight of Ben and Ignatius, its eyes rolled and it began to quiver all over. What happened next might have been a trick of the moonlight, or what happens when you should have been in bed asleep for hours, but when Ben looked at the seal again, it appeared to have turned into a girl.

## Chapter Eight

# Wild Roads

Ben blinked rapidly, in case it was a problem with his sight. But when he focused again, it was still a girl, even if it still had flippers and a rather whiskery face.

"What is it?" he said, in his alarm forgetting his manners entirely.

Iggy smirked. "The creatures of this world are so dull in comparison with those of Eidolon. This young lady is what is known in the legends of your Scottish Isles as a selkie."

Ben stared at him. "A what?"

"Must you talk about me as if I wasn't here?" the girl/seal asked suddenly. "Help me out of this box." Her voice was as musical as the sea on a calm day, and her eyes were as shiny and bright as wet beach pebbles.

Ben did as he was told and found himself clutching what appeared to be a large piece of flexible, damp black rubber. "My name"—the selkie said, coughing delicately into her other flipper—"is She Who Swims the Silver Path of the Moon, daughter of He Who Hangs Around on the Great South Rock to Attract Females; but you can call me Silver."

After a pause while he took this in, Ben replied, "I'm Ben Arnold. But my father is just called Mr. Arnold. I'm a human boy. Although Iggy here says I'm also from Eidolon, which I don't understand. What sort of creature is a selkie?"

She laughed, and her laughter was the sound of tiny waves trickling over shingle. Ben was beginning to get a bit fed up with all this sea imagery.

"I am, as this beast just explained, a child both of the water and of the air. . . ."

Out of the corner of his eye, Ben could tell that Ignatius was bridling at being called a beast. It served him right. Ben began to like the selkie better.

"I am mostly a seal who swims and plays in the briny deep, but when removed from my natural element for too long, I take on the form you see before you." She began to cough again, and now it was a terrible racking, hacking sound that made her whole body shake. "I believe," she said at last when the fit subsided, "your legends tell of magical cloaks of sealskin which, if removed, deprive the wearer of being able to change back into a sea creature." She laughed, and flung her arms wide. "Nothing so dull, as you see. Wet: a seal; dry: a girl. Well, almost. I can't seem to get my flippers to change." She clutched them to her thin chest and stared around, wide-eyed with fear. "What is this awful place? It smells of death and despair, and no magic at all. If I stay here I'll get stuck in the form of a girl, and that would be terrible. I need water to be a seal again, but if the water here is as bad as the air, it won't do me much good."

"Just like Twig," Ben said softly.

"Twig?"

Ben indicated the wood-sprite on top of the cage Iggy had been trapped in. "I found him on my lawn."

Silver gazed at Twig sorrowfully. "He certainly doesn't look well. Perhaps we are both ailing for the same reason."

Ben grimaced. "My world is bad for you?"

She shuddered. "There is no magic here," she said. "Everything feels flat and dull and lifeless. And without magic, we cannot survive."

"We'll have to find our way back into the Secret Country," Iggy added, "as soon as possible. The trouble is," he confided, "I don't know where the entrance to the correct wild road may be; and you know what they're like: We could end up anywhere if we get the wrong one."

The selkie looked at him pityingly. "Can't you cats navigate?"

"They call him the Wanderer," Ben piped up helpfully. "Because he's a great explorer."

Iggy looked embarrassed. "Well, yes. But"—he searched quickly for a face-saver—"the men who caught me knocked me over the head before I had a chance to get my bearings."

Silver looked terrified. "Then we'll die!" She

grabbed Ben by the arm with one strong flipper. Even through the sleeve of his jumper, Ben could feel the cold of another world's sea. "You must help us!"

"Whatever I can do, I will," he said simply.

"You will be my hero." The selkie closed her eyes. A vertical line appeared on her forehead, as if she was thinking very hard. "When they carried me through the way-between-worlds, the smell changed and I knew I was no longer in Eidolon. When I opened my eyes all I could see was a lot of dark bushes, a large pool of water with little colored wooden things on it, a tall rock, a winding pathway . . ."

Now it was Ben's turn to frown. Dark bushes. A large pool of water . . . a big rock . . .

The standing stone! "Aldstane Park!" he blurted out triumphantly. "The big rock—Aldstane is Old English for the Old Stone! And there's a boating lake there, and lots of trees and bushes!"

Aldstane Park lay behind King Henry Close and was the scene of many a family picnic presided over by Awful Aunt Sybil. Ben hated these outings with a passion, but he remembered one particular picnic all too well. Cousin Cynthia and his sister Ellie had made a secret camp and disappeared into the middle of the forest of rhododendrons, hollies, and hawthorns in the park, leaving Ben behind. At seven, Ben had found this both hurtful and annoying. With grim determination, he had searched for them, creeping around the bushes, tripping over roots, being startled by stray dogs. And when he at last tracked the hide-away down, the girls had ambushed him and left him tied to a tree till the moon came up and he was found by the park-keeper, who thought it all a great joke. Even now, the memory made him blush with shame.

As a hero, he had a lot of ground to make up.

Suddenly the selkie slumped to the floor, her breath sounding ragged. Iggy began to lick her face, but she pushed him feebly away. "Water . . . ," she moaned.

After a moment's thought, Ben ran downstairs. In the pet shop, the fish tanks were eerie with neon light. "Sorry," he apologized to the Mongolian Fighting Fish. He pulled off their lid, scooped the two bemused fish up in the net that hung beside the tank, and deposited them in a huge tank full of goldfish. Instead of setting about conquering this new territory with the fervor you would expect of creatures from the land of the Great Khan, they immediately swam to the bottom of the

tank and cowered, quivering with terror, beneath a
decorative arch, while the goldfish swam round and
round, staring at them, their mouths opening and closing with curiosity. Ben unplugged the empty tank and
lurched upstairs with it, water sloshing all over his
sweater. He staggered through the stockroom door and
with superhuman effort upended the contents of the
tank all over the selkie. Water went everywhere—over
the floorboards, his feet, the boxes, and the cages.
Unfortunately, quite a lot of it also went over Ignatius
Sorvo Coromandel, who yowled in outrage and leaped
for safety. From the top of a teetering stack of boxes, he
bubbled and hissed like a kettle on a stove, his fur
sleeked to his skin, not looking much like one of the
greatest feline explorers in two worlds.

At the touch of the water, Silver's skin began to
mottle and shine. She sighed and rolled, and her
movements became ever more sinuous and seal-like.
At last, rubbing her face with her flippers, she sat up.
Bristles had sprouted all round her mouth: her eyes
were round and dark.

"Thank you," was what Ben heard in his head,
though what he heard in his ears was more like a sharp
barking noise. He stared at the selkie—now definitely

more seal than girl—and wondered how on earth he was supposed to get a seal, a cat, and a wood-sprite to a park over three miles away. But even as he wondered this, the selkie was changing again: The whiskers started to recede, her head began to change shape, mottled hide gave way to skin and a thin, green cotton shift. But the flippers remained, a defiant and rubbery black.

"We'd better leave now," Ben said. "Quickly. Can you walk?"

She could, after a fashion. Ben gave the shivering Iggy a quick rubdown with his sleeve; slipped Twig, complete with baseball cap, back inside his damp sweater; grabbed up a dustsheet draped over some crates and wrapped it around Silver's head and shoulders. She looked pretty odd in it—like a rather cumbersome ghost—but, thought Ben, anything was better than being seen marching a seal around Bixbury in the middle of the night. Questions would be hard to answer.

They slipped out through the shop, leaving a frenzy of twitching noses and blinking eyes behind them. Out on the street all was silent, and even though it was the beginning of summer, there was a distinct chill in the air.

The selkie stared skyward. She smiled.

"Look!" She pointed to where a constellation rather like a saucepan with four legs and an extended handle rode the starry sky. "The Great Yeti!"

Ben followed the line of her finger and frowned. "Um, don't you mean the Great Bear?"

Silver laughed. "Not where I come from. And above it is the Pole Star."

"We call it that too!" cried Ben excitedly.

"By some strange miracle, your night sky is the same as ours," said the selkie.

They crossed the High Street and the old market square, where the moonlight fell over the war memorial. There was not another soul to be seen. The town appeared to have been abandoned, as if everyone had left suddenly to go somewhere else, been beamed up by aliens, or devoured by giant plants. Ben was visited by the unwelcome realization that Bixbury's current state somewhat echoed the growing emptiness he felt inside. Perhaps it wasn't even his true home. Perhaps he didn't belong anywhere.

He was just thinking this when there was a distant rumble. Ben stared up the road. "It's the night bus!" He ran up the street a little way and stuck his arm out.

Silver and Iggy followed uncertainly. The bus slowed and came to a halt with a screech of brakes. The automatic door opened with a sigh, and the driver stared at the motley crew at the bus stop.

"Do you go anywhere near Aldstane Park?" Ben asked.

The driver tried to peer around him at his companions.

Ben dodged sideways.

"Would King Henry Close do you?"

Ben nodded vigorously.

"Fancy-dress party, was it?" the driver asked suspiciously, still trying to get a good look at Silver and Iggy.

"Er, sort of. Two halves, please, and a cat." Ben fumbled in his pocket for the pound coin.

The driver drew himself up. "I'm afraid I don't take animals on my bus unless they're properly restrained by a leash or carried in a suitable container."

Ben stared around in anguish, but curiously there was no sign of the cat at all. Silver had edged forward and seemed to be having problems with the steps. On the pretext of helping her up, Ben leaned over and hissed, "Where's Iggy?" In response, Silver lifted a fin-

ger to her lips. Then she twitched back the volumi-
nous sheet. Iggy was clinging to the inside of it for
dear life.

Ben turned back to the driver. "Just the two halves
then, please."

Silver hauled herself up the steps, waddled past
Ben, and found herself a seat out of the driver's view.
Apart from a young couple entwined around one
another at the back, the bus was empty. When Ben
came and sat down beside the selkie, Iggy peered out
from the cloak and purred at him. Silver tucked her
flippers out of sight and gave a little smile.

Ten minutes later, the bus dropped them off on the
corner of King Henry Close. But when they reached
Aldstane Park, the gates were locked. Ben rattled them
uselessly. He tried to shimmy up the tall railings on
either side, but each time slipped back down, burning
his palms. "What shall we do?" Silver wailed. Her
voice tailed off into a haunting, dolphinlike cry. She
slumped to the pavement, coughing.

Iggy wove around her in disconsolate figures-of-
eight, mewing, "Now, now, She Who Swims the Silver
Path of the Moon, don't worry, Ben will think of
something."

At this, Twig began to stir too. Ben took him out of his sweater and laid him on the ground between them. The wood-sprite seemed listless. He kept twisting around in the baseball cap as if he couldn't find a comfortable position.

Ben sat down with his chin on his knees, feeling responsibility pressing down upon him. He remembered what his mother had said, that looking after other creatures taught you responsibility—which was all very well; but what it didn't teach you was what to do at times like this. He was out of his depth here. He looked up, about to admit defeat. In the moonlight, Silver's skin and hair appeared colorless. Now she really looked like a ghost. For a moment, Ben found himself wondering if he were dreaming all this; then she put a flipper on his shoulder, and again he felt the strange coolness, as if someone had draped seaweed upon him. "You will think of something," she said between coughs. "I know it, Ben Arnold."

It was as if the saying of his name gave Ben the power he needed to solve the problem.

"Can you climb?" he asked the selkie.

Silver smiled. "I will follow you anywhere."

Ben jumped up and pulled her to her feet. "Come on," he said. "I have an idea!"

At the western wall of the park stood a great ash tree, with branches that swept low on either side of the fence. The ash lay silhouetted against the sky like Yggdrasil the World Tree from Ben's favorite book of Norse legends, the tree whose roots lay in the under-world and whose branches swept the heavens. *Had the ancient peoples somehow known there was another world, a secret country, touching our own?* Ben wondered.

He stowed the sprite in his sweater again, grabbed hold of one of the low-slung branches, and swung himself up. It was surprising to see that all that gym-work was really beginning to pay off. Perhaps there were other aspects of school that might yet come in handy, though it seemed unlikely.

Iggy leaped past him, ran lightly to the junction with the trunk, and sat there, smiling smugly. It was a bit of a struggle (he had no idea that a selkie could be so heavy), but Ben managed to haul Silver up beside him. They edged along the branch and stared down the other side of the fence. The selkie cried out in sudden delight. Stretching away from them in the moonlight was the boating lake, shining like a mirror in the center of the park. Ben helped Silver to clamber along the branches, and when they reached a great down-swooping branch on the park side of the ash, Iggy and Ben jumped to the ground.

Silver lay on her stomach across the branch and looked down. "I'm not sure I can jump so far."

Ben grimaced. He placed Twig carefully between the roots of the ash tree and went to stand beneath Silver, arms outstretched.

The selkie wriggled awkwardly into a sitting position and swung her hind flippers over the side of the branch. A bout of coughing made her double up in pain. When she opened her eyes again, they were watery with what might have been tears.

"Just let go and I'll catch you," Ben said with a confidence he didn't feel.

Silver shut her eyes and pushed herself away from the branch. As if in sympathy, Ben found his own eyes shutting. He waited for the impact, but none came. Instead there was a rush of movement, followed by the sound of tearing fabric, and then a soft thump. He opened his eyes to find the torn sheet hanging from a snag on the branch, and Silver, her fall broken by the ripping cotton, safe and sound beside him.

"Luck is clearly running with us," Iggy breathed.

Silver took one look at the boating lake and started to lumber toward the shining water. Her flippers slapped against the grass. At the edge of the lake, she slipped out of her sea green shift and a moment later there was a splash. The water closed seamlessly over the selkie's head. The moon shone down on the dark surface and traced in silver the progress of the concentric ripples spreading away to the shore. Ben held his breath. At last there was a disturbance beneath the surface and something reappeared. It was not the head of the girl who had gone in, but of a seal, slippery and whiskery and liquid-eyed. The seal dived and resurfaced, dived and resurfaced. It swam with a sinuous, lithe grace that filled Ben with envy.

Iggy, however, watched the display with a look of disgust. "Ugh, water," he said, and turned away, shuddering.

At last the seal swept across the lake, flopped inelegantly out onto the shore, and blinked its large, wet, round eyes at them.

Even in the cool of the night, the water began to evaporate at once. Ben watched in amazement as the water dried; for where there had been sleek, mottled sealskin, areas of pale pink were beginning to show through. The seal reached a flipper to the scrap of sea green fabric on the ground, and as she did so the flipper began to lengthen and refine its shape and eventually become an arm, albeit with a rather blurred, dark mass on the end that was neither quite flipper nor hand. Ben was so mesmerized by this transformation that he missed the exact moment when seal became girl. When he looked up again Silver was fully clothed and gazing at him with a delighted smile. She was, he realized suddenly, quite beautiful, with her pale hair and her huge eyes restored to some vestige of health.

"Thank you," she said.

"It was nothing. It's not much of a lake," Ben replied.

"Not for that, though I am grateful indeed. No, I thank you for your chivalry."

"My what?"

"For not staring at me unclothed."

"Oh, that." He hadn't even thought to do so. "No problem."

"You are a true friend, Ben Arnold."

Ben felt himself go pink with pleasure.

Feeling rather left out in this exchange, Iggy cleared his throat. "And what about this wild road?" he said.

The selkie smiled at Ben and he felt as if his heart had grown to twice its normal size. She stared up into the night sky, then turned around. "Over there, among those bushes."

Ben followed the line of her arm to a great forest of irregular black shapes. He shivered. He remembered those bushes well. "Are you sure?"

The selkie nodded.

Ignatius Sorvo Coromandel interposed himself between them. "Better let me go first. The eyes, you know." And indeed his eyes were glowing like headlights in the moonlight.

They followed him into the midst of the rhododendrons. Beneath the canopy of leaves it was very dark, and cooler than it was in the open. Ben held Iggy's tail with one hand; Twig twisted and turned on the baseball cap in his other hand; and Silver brought up the rear, holding on to Ben's jumper and shuffling noisily along amongst the dry leaves; and in this strange configuration they wove between the shrubs and bushes for several minutes.

At last Iggy stopped.

"What?" said Ben.

"Er, nothing," Iggy said, rather uncertainly, and led off again.

Some minutes later they found themselves back in the same place.

"We've been here before," said Silver.

"I thought they called you the Wanderer because you were a great navigator," Ben exclaimed, rather crossly.

"Hmmm. Yes," said Iggy, and did not elaborate.

He sniffed the ground with an air of scientific precision, then led them off in a different direction. They ducked under branches and suddenly found themselves in a small circular clearing.

As they did so, a weird red illumination sprang up around them, painting their faces and the undersides of the trees with a wash of scarlet. Iggy's eyes flared like a demon's. Silver gave out a tiny shriek of alarm, and Ben gazed wildly around, trying to determine the source of the phenomenon. The light was suddenly accompanied by a scratchy, high-pitched humming, rather like the whine of a giant mosquito. Ben stared at his hand. It was Twig. The little wood-sprite was sitting bolt upright, his whole body vibrating like a tuning fork. He was singing. The strange red light shone out from every pore of his body. It fled away from the wood-sprite, out along the dusty ground like a running fuse, sparking off roots and dead leaves, until at last it lit up against a great slab of rock partially hidden among a grove of hawthorns.

Ignatius Sorvo Coromandel grinned, and his teeth flashed as red as blood. "You see? I've found the entrance to the wild road." He bent his head and began to sniff energetically along the path of the light. When he reached the rock, he came to a halt. He walked three times around it, stepping carefully in and out of the thorny bushes, then stopped and walked back the other way. "It's the one," he declared. "No doubt about it."

Silver shuffled forward. "Let me see." She dropped to all fours, then gave a whoop of delight, which was followed by another coughing fit.

"What is it?" Ben was at her side at once.

Iggy craned his neck, ever curious.

The selkie was fiddling with a branch of hawthorn. Caught on the thorns was a scrap of red fabric. "Help me," she said breathlessly.

Ben folded the wood-sprite back into the baseball cap and slipped him down inside his sweater. The red light subsided to a gentle glow, and the strip of cloth changed color to a pale pinky-green. Ben disentangled it from the hawthorn and held it out to Silver.

"It's from my dress!"

She twirled around to show Ben and Iggy the back of the flimsy sea green tunic. Near the hem there was a small zigzag of fabric missing, as if torn violently away. The scrap she held fitted the hole perfectly.

"Wow," said Ben, overwhelmed.

"This is where they carried me through to your world," she said. "This is where I was imprisoned in the box."

"It's where I came in too," said the cat. He gave a low growl. "There are human footmarks here, and I remember the smell of the stone."

Ben ran his hands over the rock. It was pitted with age and patched with lichen and was sunk deep in the earth, deep in the leaf mold. It seemed that, like an iceberg, there was more of it below the ground than appeared above. Ben's fingers traveled across it as if remembering something. He stopped, then took Twig out of his sweater. Holding the wood-sprite close to the rock like a torch, he examined the surface closely.

Obscured by lichen and the corrosion of rain, a pattern was still visible. Someone had carved a word into the stone. It consisted of a lot of straight lines and angles, and for a while Ben could not quite make it out. Then . . . "Look!"

They crowded around.

"It's the Old Stone!" Ben exclaimed. "It's a sort of way-marker. . . ." His fingers traced the marks as he spelled them out: "E-I-D-O-L-O-N." And someone had rather more recently chalked an arrow on the Aldstane, pointing down into the ground.

Ignatius Sorvo Coromandel stepped around to the back of the stone, where the hawthorns made a dark hollow. There he did something with a front foot. It disappeared. Ben stared. Iggy pressed his face close to the ground where his foot had gone. A second later, his head had disappeared as well.

Ben's breath hissed out in alarm.

A few seconds later, the cat reemerged intact. "I can smell it!" he cried. "I can smell our home!"

The wood-sprite was sitting up now, his huge prismatic eyes gleaming red, like raspberries lit from within. All his deathlike lethargy had dispersed with the possibility of returning to the Secret Country. He looked . . . well—*spritely*, Ben thought. Then he thought, How did people know what spritely meant, when there were no sprites in this world?

This pondering was interrupted by Silver tapping him on the shoulder. "Come with us, Ben Arnold," she said.

The cat stood poised on the edge of the wild road.

"Come with us to Eidolon, Ben," Iggy exhorted. "Come and learn your destiny."

The Secret Country: a place filled with magic and wonders; a world that was in some way also his own; a world that bordered his like a shadow. A world that could be entered only by a wild road. Ben shivered. Did he really want to go to such a place? What if he couldn't get back again? Would he start to ail as Twig and Silver were ailing in his world?

Iggy started to shuffle impatiently.

Ben thought of his family. He thought of his sisters: Ellie, so sarcastic and touchy, who had, for all her faults, saved up and bought him the perfect gift— *Fish: The Ultimate Encyclopedia*—for Christmas last year; baby Alice, who would clutch his finger in her tiny hand as if her powerful grasp was the only way she could communicate her love. He thought of his father: so busy with his job on the paper, cracking jokes as he did the dishes; his father, who had volunteered to cut all of Awful Uncle Aleister's hedges in exchange for a fish tank to make Ben happy. And then he thought of his mother. He did not think of her exhausted and wheelchair-bound, but of the brightness of her green eyes, the quirk of that single raised eyebrow before she dropped him one of her slow, conspiratorial winks.

"I can't leave them," he thought. "I just can't."

Then he realized he had spoken these words out loud, for Silver had burst into tears. She came to him and hugged him. He felt her strange coldness around him, and it was like being at sea.

"I know that I will see you again, Ben Arnold."

Ben nodded mutely. He couldn't speak, since a huge lump had risen in his throat.

Twig, his red light at last extinguished, flew up in front of Ben's face, dragging the baseball cap. It was clearly a great effort, but the wood-sprite was smiling, showing two rows of glittering, sharp teeth. He deposited the cap (slug slime and shepherd's pie remnants and all) on Ben's head. "Thank you, Ben . . .

saved me . . . never forget . . ." Then he fell to the ground with a thump, exhausted.

The selkie bent and picked Twig up gently in her great dark flippers and cradled him against her chest.

Ignatius Sorvo Coromandel dragged himself away from the entrance to the wild road. "Are you quite sure that you will not come with us, Ben?"

Ben nodded, and a single tear squeezed itself out of one eye. He rubbed it away angrily. "I'm sorry, Iggy. I can't. My mother's ill. I can't leave her."

The little cat looked sad. "Eidolon is your destiny, Ben, and I would like to show you your other home."

Ben smiled, a little lopsidedly. "Even so."

Iggy rubbed his head against Ben's leg and a huge purr rumbled through the grove. Ben dropped to one knee and held the cat against him so hard, he could feel its heart beating against his hands. "I will miss you, Iggy."

In the darkness, the little cat grinned. "I own your true name, Benjamin Christopher Arnold," he said in his gravelly cowboy voice. "I can call you anytime." Then Iggy disengaged himself and stood before the entrance to the wild road. He looked back over his shoulder at Ben and reminded him, "And you have my true name and can do the same. Though you can do it only three times, so don't waste it!" Then, like the Cheshire Cat, he disappeared gradually from sight, until not even a grin was left behind.

Silver leaned forward suddenly and kissed Ben's cheek.

Then she stepped behind the Aldstane and vanished.

Ben stood there alone in the dark for a long time, rubbing the cool trace of the selkie's lips against his cheek. Then he turned, parted the bushes, and came out once more into the park. The moonlight showed the pattern of their path across the dewy grass as a snaking, dark trail. He followed it to the oak tree, climbed back to the road, and began the long walk home.

## *The London Daily Tribune*

### UFO seen over Parliament

Late-night pedestrians crossing Westminster Bridge reported sightings of an unidentified object flying across the face of Big Ben.

"It was much larger than any normal bird," said Paula Smith (34), a practicing herbalist. "I've never seen anything like it."

A group of Japanese tourists took several

photographs of the object. It is somewhat indistinct, caught between the illuminated face of the clock tower and the light of the full moon, but it is the opinion of this newspaper that the object is probably either a heron or the result of a hoax.

Professor Arthur James Dyer from London University's Department of Extinct Animals disagrees.

"It's certainly a great deal bigger than a heron, and the set of the wings is not obviously avian. As far as I'm concerned, there's no doubt about it: it's the first clear sighting of a live pterodactyl."

This is not an isolated incident. There have been several instances in recent weeks of witnesses purporting to have seen unusual creatures in the vicinity of our capital city.

Last Tuesday, revelers on Hampstead Heath saw what they described as a large, dark, hairy animal running into the undergrowth on the eastern edge of the heath. One of the witnesses stated that he had had a very clear view and that the creature had "the head and torso of a horned man" and the "legs and nether regions of a goat." It was, he claimed, "quite clearly a satyr."

This sighting has generally been dismissed as the work of a fancy-dress trickster.

## *The Kernow Herald*

## LOCAL MAN IN HOSPITAL

### The Beast of Bodmin:
### Fact or Fiction?

Ramblers returning from a walk around the Sibleyback Reservoir on Bodmin Moor on Sunday morning scattered and ran for their cars when surprised by a loud roaring noise from behind a drystone wall.

Mr. B. Wise of Daglands Road, Fowey, did not live up to his name by staying in his vehicle. His wife, Barbara, blonde, 43, recounted for us her version of events:

"There was this terrible roaring, and Bernard said to me, 'That's the Beast, that is. I'm going to get some piccies for the newspapers and make my fortune.' The next thing I know, he's grabbed his camcorder and slipped out of the car. Then he started climbing the wall. My Bernard's never been that fit, but he got nearly to the top and—well, what happened next was a bit of a blur. I saw a large black shape rearing up, and then a chunk of the wall came off in Bernard's hand and he fell over backward and hit his head. I got him to Emergency at Callington Hospital, but he's been out cold ever since."

A hospital spokesperson told us that Mr. Wise is now out of Intensive Care and is "as well as can be expected." Nurse Samantha Ramsay added, off the record, that he was probably lucky that the wall had got him rather than what was behind it.

There have been stories about a "Beast on the Moors" for decades now, but in the last month rumors have spread like wildfire. There have been over twenty reported sightings of what is believed to be a very big cat, and local farmers have lost a number of sheep. Experts called in from London Zoo's Conservation of Dangerous Animals Department examined the remains of some of the victims and were surprised by what they found.

"We thought it might be an escaped puma or leopard," said Dr. Ivor Jones. "But really, the width of jaw indicated by the bite marks suggests a very much larger animal, probably with enormous canine teeth, possibly even as large as those of a smilodon."

Since smilodons (saber-toothed tigers) became extinct during the Tertiary period, and there is no living cat with a similar bite pattern, Dr. Jones's opinions have provoked considerable controversy.

# Part Two

# There

## Chapter Nine

# At Awful Uncle Aleister's

In the days that followed, Ben regretted his decision not to follow his companions to the Secret Country. He thought about it when he was awake, his mind wandered in class, and at night he saw Iggy and Twig and Silver in his dreams: a small black and brown cat with shiny golden eyes staring out across an unfamiliar landscape from the top of a stone tower; a wood-sprite, grinning from ear to ear, chasing dozy moths in and out of the branches in a dark forest. Most of all he dreamed of She Who Swims the Silver Path of the Moon, swimming with a lazy flick of her tail from the murky ocean depths to the surface of a shining sea.

But some nights his dreams were less serene. Once he dreamed of a terrible tall figure stalking across the land, its huge dog-head silhouetted against the moon, its sharp white teeth glinting in the pale light; and he heard the cries of terrified creatures dwindling to moans as if they were being dragged down some great, long tunnel.

Sometimes when he woke from these nightmares, it was to the sound of his baby sister wailing in the dark, and a vague sense that he was guilty of something, as if there was some important task he had left undone.

At school he tried to put such thoughts behind him, but in every class something would crop up to remind him of the Secret Country: In English they were given an essay entitled "Imagine your pet was suddenly given the power of speech"; in technical drawing they drew bisecting circles that made Ben think of the moment Iggy had described of Eidolon being jolted away from Earth; and in biology when Mr. Soames told them about the dinosaurs being dead, Ben, unthinking, piped up with, "No they're not, sir: they live in . . ."

Luckily his mate Adam saved him from further embarrassment by adding ". . . Transylvania!" which made the rest of the class laugh and jeer.

Ben was desperate to tell someone about his adventures. The pressure of his secrets was building up inside him until he thought he would burst. He'd thought of saying something to Ellie, but he knew she'd shriek with laughter, tell all her snotty friends (particularly Cousin Cynthia, with whom she was thick as thieves), and tease him mercilessly about it. His father was more preoccupied than usual. Mr. Arnold told Ben he was "onto something that could turn out to be a big story" and spent a lot of time out of the house doing "research." Several times he came close to telling his mother; but she seemed so tired and ill that although she was the most likely member of the family to believe him, he felt sure it would just make her worry about him, and that would make her even more tired. So he'd gone out one morning, looked around to make sure no one could hear him, and approached the thin white cat with the slanting eyes.

"Look," he'd said in as reasonable a fashion as he

could manage, "I've got to talk to someone about this or I'll go mad. You're a cat; you're supposed to know about Eidolon and the Wanderer and wild roads and stuff. Is it true, or did I dream it all?"

The cat gave him a sharp, rebuking look, then arched her back and stalked away.

*Well*, thought Ben. *How rude*. Then he thought, *Perhaps she's a bit deaf.* He shouted after her, but she slunk under the fence and disappeared. So either his ability to converse with animals had evaporated along with Ignatius Sorvo Coromandel, or he'd imagined the whole episode.

But who would make up a name like that? Who in their right mind would concoct such an unlikely tale?

When he went back into the house, his mother called his name. She was in the kitchen, slumped in her wheelchair. The clothes she had been trying to load into the washing machine lay strewn across the floor.

"Oh, Ben," she said when she saw him, and her voice had a defeated air.

The jeans he had worn on the night he had taken Iggy and Twig and Silver to Aldstane Park lay across her knees, and she was holding something small and dark in her hand. Her face looked pale and drawn and her eyes had a faraway look, but her voice was fraught with anger.

"Where did you get this?"

She opened her hand. The object she held was brown and almost oval in shape, and one end was sharper than the other. There were small wrinkles and striations on one side, while the underside appeared smooth. It looked like a piece of fir cone, but whatever it was made of wasn't wood. It took some moments before he could remember where he'd found it.

"Well? I'm waiting for an answer, Ben."

How could he tell his mother that he'd broken into Mr. Dodds's Pet Emporium and found this strange thing on the stockroom floor? He knew that although his mother hated cruelty to any creature and would be horrified to hear about Mr. Dodds's terrible trade, she would be very angry with him.

"I . . . I don't know what it is," he said, hoping to deflect her.

"Ah, but I do, and it shouldn't be in this world at all." She closed her eyes as if overcome with exhaustion. "Too late," she whispered. "I should have gone back, but I left it too late. . . ."

Ben felt his heart contract. "What is it, Mum? Are you okay?"

Mrs. Arnold gave her son an anguished look, tried to wheel herself toward the back door, and collapsed.

Ben dropped to his knees beside his mother. "Mum, what's the matter?"

Her eyes flickered over him, but she didn't seem to see him. Her mouth moved as if she was saying something, but no sound came out.

Ben felt helpless. He caught up his mother's wrist, and the object fell from her hand. He stuffed it back in his pocket, then found her pulse and counted, just like they had taught him to do in the first aid course at school.

One hundred and fifty. That couldn't be right.

The next time he tried it was two hundred. Ben rushed out into the hall. Should he call an ambulance, or his father? In the end he did both.


No one knew what was wrong with her. At the hospital they kept her in isolation and hooked her up to all sorts of tubes, but she got no better. A friend of hers came and took baby Alice away. Awful Uncle Aleister and Aunt Sybil offered to look after Ben and Ellie so that Mr. Arnold could spend time at his wife's bedside.

"Dad . . . ," Ben began pleadingly, but his father turned a face full of misery to him, and after that he couldn't refuse.

"It'll only be for a week or so, till she's over the worst of it," Mr. Arnold said, as if he believed it.

It was awful at Awful Uncle Aleister's. Ben had known it would be, with a sort of vague dread that failed to focus on specific details. Imagination had never been his strong point, and so he was very unprepared for what was to come. First of all, Aunt Sybil took his shoes away from him at the door before letting him inside ("mustn't spoil the carpets"); then she made him have a bath and wash his hair with some vile-smelling concoction that would, she promised with a nervous laugh, "get rid of any nasty little unwelcome visitors."

Ben had no idea what she meant by this, though the idea of visitors in his hair, partying away, having a good time, invisible to the rest of the world, was rather appealing. Even so, he did what he was told, though the shampoo made his eyes water and his scalp sting. It was only when Cynthia sneered at him and said something about lice that he realized what Aunt Sybil had meant, and after that his head itched all night.

He had been given a supper of kidneys and boiled potatoes and stewed cabbage that had tasted so awful he couldn't eat it, despite being ravenous, and as a result he had been sent to bed early with his plate of horrid food, to what Aunt Sybil called "the box room." He supposed that was because there were a lot of boxes in it. So many boxes, in fact, that there was hardly room for a bed. They were brown cardboard boxes, and they were piled high in a higgledy-piggledy sort of way. None of them were labeled, and all were bound with brown packing tape. The first one he tried to lift was so heavy he couldn't move it; but the next was oddly light, as if someone had taped up a boxful of air. When he shook it, he could hear nothing inside.

He sat on the edge of the rickety camp bed and stared at the plate. Then, slowly, he ate all the potatoes. But the cabbage was gray and slippery and smelled like old pondwater; and as for the kidneys . . . Defeated, he found a plastic bag and shoveled the rest of the food into it, then stowed the bag in his rucksack.

Tomorrow he would smuggle it out to the bins before Aunt Sybil found out. Then he thought about sawing open one of the boxes with the penknife Aunt Sybil and Uncle Aleister had failed to confiscate from him, but decided they might keep feeding him kidneys and cabbage if they found out. Or worse. Then, for a long while, he thought about his mother. Tears threatened. To distract himself, he took the odd object he had picked up at the pet shop out of the pocket of his jeans and turned it over and over in his fingers, feeling its strange serrations and the smooth curve of its inside face. He was holding it at arm's length and wondering just why his mother had been so affected by it when the door came slightly ajar and a creature appeared at the foot of it. It was a small and hairless creature with a pointy face and large ears and uptilted eyes of amber yellow. Wrinkles of skin pooled around its feet and bagged at its joints. Nudging the door harder with its head, it came into the room and stood there, staring at him. Ben was so surprised by the sight of it that he dropped the thing he had been holding. It skittered across the uncarpeted floor and came to rest in front of the hairless creature, which stepped back nervously. Then it took a step closer and sniffed it. Its head shot up in alarm. At last it bashed the object with its paw and hissed so that its face became one big wrinkle.

It was then that Ben realized this strange creature must be a cat: to be precise, Cynthia's new cat. But cats were supposed to have silky coats from head to toe. What new atrocity had Cynthia subjected the poor beast to?

He put out his hand. "Here, Kitty, Kitty," he said softly.

The cat—or whatever it was—gave him an evil look.

"Don't 'Kitty' me," it said, its voice high and scratchy.

Ben grinned. "You can talk! I was beginning to think I'd imagined all that. What's your name?"

The cat smiled. "You won't catch me like that." It stalked across the room, squinted up at him, then leaped up onto the windowsill behind him. Ben could feel its eyes on him like a cold shadow on the back of his neck. He shivered and turned around.

"Are you a cat? What happened to your fur?"

"So many questions."

"Did Cynthia do something to you? She doesn't always look after her pets—"

The cat hissed at him. "Petssss? I am no pet. I am a Sphynx."

Ben raised his eyebrows. It sounded pretty impressive, but the only sphinxes he knew were the ones that guarded the Great Pyramid of Cheops, and this wizened, wrinkly little beast looked more like Yoda than a grand Egyptian carving.

As if it could read his mind, the cat rolled its eyes. "We Sphynxes are hairlesss, not covered in smelly fur like common catsss." It looked sly. "Unlike the Wanderer."

"You know the Wanderer?"

The Sphynx began to groom a paw in a peculiarly catlike fashion. "Oh, yesss, I know the Wanderer." It examined its spread toes, then lifted innocent eyes to Ben. "You don't happen to know where he isss, do you?"

"No. The last time I saw him—" Ben stopped. "Why do you want to know?"

"He'sss a . . . friend."

Something about the way the Sphynx said this made Ben doubt the truth of this statement. "Er, he went wandering," he finished lamely.

The cat regarded him suspiciously.

"In Eidolon," Ben added, to test the creature's reaction.

The Sphynx's ears went flat to its skull. "Sssssssssss! What do you know about the Shadow World?"

"Oh, this and that," Ben said airily. "How to get there—that sort of thing."

Now the cat looked fearful. It jumped down from the windowsill and slunk around the edge of the room as if keeping as much distance as possible between itself and Ben. "She'sss sent you as her sssspy," it muttered. "I should have known." It narrowed its eyes at him. "You should not involve yourssself in thingsss that do not concern you, Ben Arnold. It could be very dangerousss."

And with that, it disappeared.

Ben sat on the bed for a while, feeling distinctly uncomfortable. He wished Iggy were there to talk to. Then he got up, crept over to the door, and peered around it down the corridor. There was no sign of the Sphynx, nor of anyone else. Closing the door quietly, he picked up the thing he had taken from Mr. Dodds's stockroom and stared at it again.

It looked so ordinary, but the cat had seemed frightened by it.

And he remembered how his mother had reacted when she had found it in his jeans pocket.

What on earth could it be?

He turned it over and examined the underside, but got no more clues from that. He rubbed it between his fingers and found it rough on one side and smooth on the other. Under closer scrutiny it looked as if it might once have been a reddish color, but it had somehow faded to this rather uninteresting brown. He sniffed at it, and it smelled slightly musty, like something that had once been alive.

Frowning, he climbed into bed and tried to get comfortable. His thoughts circled around his mind like bats in a cave.

Ben slept badly that night. It might have been because the camp bed's mattress was so lumpy. It might have been because he was in Awful Uncle Aleister's house. It might have been because he was hungry, or because Cynthia and Ellie were giggling away in the room next door. Or it might have been because of what the Sphynx had said.

At any rate, he found himself suddenly wide awake in the dead hours of the morning. Outside, an engine was running, low and rumbly. He got up and peered through the window. A truck had backed up into the driveway. Its tailgate was open, as if someone were loading or unloading from it. Ben squinted into the darkness. For a long time he could see nothing at all, for there was no moon; but he had the sense of there being a lot of activity, for he could hear the scuffle of footsteps on the gravel and even a murmur of voices. A few minutes later his patience was rewarded when something moved close to the house and the security light came on. Two figures with hooked noses, hunched bodies, and clawed fingers . . .

The security light went off.

Ben sucked in his breath, blinked, blinked again. He rubbed his eyes. Surely he hadn't seen what he thought he'd seen? But the light did not come on again, and a little while later he heard the trunk being banged shut, then someone climbed into the cab and drove the truck out into the road. He watched as its red brake lights dwindled into the distance.

Perhaps he was still dreaming. That would explain everything.

But as he moved away from the window he stubbed his toe on the bed leg, which made him painfully aware that he wasn't dreaming at all.

And that the figures he had seen loading boxes into the back of the truck really had been a pair of goblins.

## Chapter Ten

# A Remarkable Discovery

At breakfast the next morning Ben found that Cynthia was watching him warily, which was unusual, since she rarely looked at him at all except to glare. Even Ellie seemed subdued. This meant that the conversation was left to Awful Uncle Aleister and Aunt Sybil, who were planning some sort of outing. Ben wasn't paying much attention—partly because the subject sounded really very dull (a customer had been complaining about some faulty goods the company had supplied) and partly because Cynthia's cat, the unnamed Sphynx, was sitting right on top of the bookcase like a particularly unpleasant bookend, staring at him with its unblinking yellow eyes.

"Well, what do you think?" Aunt Sybil asked brightly. "Shall we all make a day of it?"

Uncle Aleister did not seem too happy at the idea of the entire family accompanying him on his errand. "You'd be very bored," he kept saying.

"But," said Aunt Sybil forcefully, "I believe the house is one of the finest examples of Tudor architecture in the country. It would do the children good to acquire a bit of culture."

Her husband rolled his eyes. He knew when he was beaten.

"Is there a shop?" The girls wondered. It was all Ellie and Cynthia were interested in.

Aunt Sybil smiled and avoided the question. "It has lovely grounds. And a knot garden."

Cynthia curled her lip. "Do I look like someone who cares about knots?" she snarled.

"And some very famous Whistlers."

Now even Ellie was rude enough to snort with

laughter. "Who wants to listen to some idiots whistling?"

Aunt Sybil became flustered. "No, no, dear—they're paintings. . . ."

Of course that didn't do the trick either.

Ben, who had for a moment been quite curious about a team of whistlers, found his attention straying back to the goblins he had seen last night. What had they been doing here, at Uncle Aleister's? It was all very odd. Rather than go to some crumbling country house full of musty furniture and old paintings, he thought he'd rather stay behind and search for clues. And he wanted another chance to talk to the Sphynx.

"Right then, no more arguments from you lot!" Uncle Aleister announced. "We're all going and that's an end to it. Chop, chop! We can't keep Lady Hawley-Fawley waiting."

Ben's ears pricked up. "Would that be Lady Hawley-Fawley of Crawley?" he ventured.

Awful Uncle Aleister regarded him disdainfully. "What on earth would a boy like you know about the aristocracy?"

Ben floundered. "Er . . . I . . ." He thought desperately, then said the first thing that came into his head. "I hear she has a world-famous collection of shoes."

Why on earth had he said *that*?

"Shoes?" Ellie's face lit up.

"Fantastic," said Cynthia.

And that was that. Half an hour later they all piled into Aunt Sybil's Range Rover and drove to Crawley.

All the way there, Ben tried to remember exactly how he knew Lady Hawley-Fawley's name. It wasn't as if he'd ever met any lords or ladies. Perhaps his father had mentioned her when working on one of his stories for the newspaper. But that didn't sound right either. It was only when Uncle Aleister said something to his wife about the faulty item being a garden incinerator that something clicked into place.

He remembered a letter with an embossed crest lying on the desk in the Pet Emporium's office. But that letter had been addressed to Mr. Dodds.

So if that was the case . . .

He stared very hard at the back of Awful Uncle Aleister's head and thought about the implications.

● ● ●

Rather than follow the rest of them into the grand mansion, Ben made an excuse of wanting to explore the gardens instead. To his surprise, no one argued with him. Uncle Aleister had his appointment, and Aunt Sybil, Cousin Cynthia, and Ellie were far too excited about the famous shoe collection to mind that he was going off on his own. Which was another good reason to disappear for a while.

First of all, he saw a sign for the knot garden and went to have a look, but it was a rather disappointing affair made up of low green hedges and colored gravel, and there was no sign of any knots at all. The fountains were turned off and some fat pigeons were sitting around the edges, looking bored. He followed the path past the ornamental ponds where fat orange goldfish meandered lazily through the weed like miniature submarines, and found himself at last in an orchard. Last year's leaves were strewn on the grass between the fruit trees, making the area untidier than the rest of the grounds, but Ben preferred the wildness here. He kicked some leaves around and watched the way they spiraled in the breeze. He picked up a fallen apple and, after giving it a cursory polish on his jeans, bit into it; but the fruit was tart and unripe, and when he looked into the bite mark he'd made, he spied something white and wriggly near the core. "Ugh! Maggots!" He threw the apple away from him as hard as he could and walked on.

Beyond the orchard was an area of trampled grass and scattered brown objects that crunched underfoot like the dried husks of beechnuts. Within feet, the trampled grass gave on to an even scruffier area where rusting machinery, bales of hay, rolls of wire netting, and tree-stakes lay tumbled between weathered sheds and lichen-streaked outhouses. There were broken plant pots, bags of rotting compost, and garden implements. Old crates, a bicycle missing its front wheel; and a dragon.

Ben came to a halt, his eyes bulging.

He had never seen a dragon before, except in books. There, they were sheathed in glorious color, breathing sheets of fire that turned maidens to Kentucky Fried Chicken in seconds flat. Or fighting bold knights who had come to slay them. Or curled around hoards of gold in mountain caves, guarding their treasure from thieves. They were creatures from the world of legend, powerful, cruel, and magnificent, soaring and swooping in the twilight skies of mythology.

This dragon did not look as if it had ever soared, or fought a knight, or even cooked a maiden. It was small (for a dragon), and it had a heavy collar around its neck, which someone had tied to a fence post with a length of frayed rope. It sat hunched up with its scaly tail and a pair of thin, leathery wings curled around its feet like a domestic cat. Its hide was patched and mottled. Its head hung down dejectedly. It did not even look up as he approached.

"Hello," said Ben.

The dragon lifted its head very slowly, as if the weight of it was more than it could manage.

Its eyes were purple and seemed to have several rings of iris rather than the usual one. Ben felt that if he were to stare into them for any length of time he would become very confused indeed.

When it saw that its visitor was a mere boy, the dragon hung its head again and sat there contemplating its long, scaly toes.

Ben walked up to it cautiously. He knew he should feel afraid, since the dragons in the books he had read had been terrifying monsters, but all he felt for this one was curiosity and a sort of pity. The dragon looked not only unthreatening, but defeated, and rather sad. He wanted to hug it. He wanted to untie it from its post and set it free.

His fingers closed around the thing in his pocket, and suddenly he knew exactly what it was.

"Excuse me," he started again, it seeming a good idea to be as polite as possible. "Is this yours by any chance?"

He took the scale out of his pocket, held his hand under the creature's nose, and watched as its nostrils flared. Then two little protuberances on top of its head, which he imagined might be ears, started to twitch. He took a step back, just in case it was preparing to barbecue him.

"Another one," the dragon said gloomily.

"I beg your pardon?"

"You found another one, then," the dragon repeated.

It nodded its head around in a vague sort of way, and Ben knew he'd been right. The things that looked like husks of dried nuts were scales that had fallen off into the trodden grass and dust, and the mottled effect of the dragon's coat was because many of the scales had peeled away in patches, exposing areas of gray-brown hide. Even those that remained were dull and dead-looking.

"Are you ill?" he asked suddenly. "You don't look very well."

"I'm very tired," the dragon said slowly. It fixed Ben with its strange eyes. "And I'm very hungry."

Ben laughed nervously. "Don't they feed you, then?"

The dragon wearily lifted a front foot and indicated a pile of cabbage leaves and potato peelings rotting away by one of the sheds. "If you can call that food."

"What would you prefer? Perhaps I can get it for you."

The eyes flashed for a second. "I was always rather partial to the odd warm-blooded mammal," the dragon said. It assessed him slowly. Then it gave him a crocodile smile. "Lucky for you I don't have the strength to roast a rabbit at the moment. Or even a dingbat."

"A what?"

But the dragon was staring off into the distance, looking wistful.

Ben had an idea. He took off his rucksack. Inside was the plastic bag containing last night's congealed supper. He had meant to put it in a bin, but now he upended it in front of the dragon. "You might like some of this," he suggested, though it was hard to imagine that anyone would, even a starving creature from another world.

The dragon sniffed at the gooey pile. It nosed about in it for a bit, separating the cabbage from the meat. Then a long gray tongue—just like a snake's, but much, much bigger—shot out, and two seconds later all the kidneys were gone.

The dragon regarded him hopefully. "Mmmm," it said. "That was delicious. Is there any more?"

Food in the Secret Country was obviously a lot less appetizing than food in this world, Ben decided, remembering how ravenously Iggy had scoffed the shepherd's pie.

"No," he said. "Sorry. That's all there is."

He was just thinking about how excellent it would be to hide the dragon in Awful Uncle Aleister's garden to dispose of his unwanted dinners, when he heard voices. Two people were coming through the orchard, and by the sound of his booming voice, one of them was Uncle Aleister.

Ben grimaced. Then he grabbed up his rucksack and the plastic bag and fled around the back of the nearest shed. Behind him, he heard the dragon mutter, "Very rude. Really, how very rude. Not even a good-bye. Or, in fact, an introduction . . ."

"It's completely useless, I tell you," came the voice that was not Uncle Aleister's. "It's not worked properly since Day One. All it does is sit there and look miserable—as you can see it's not burned a single leaf in all the time I've had it. The orchard's a disgrace! I can't even show the thing orf to my guests, it's so ugly; and I'm quaite sure it's sick, for as you'll perceive, all its scales are falling orf."

The speaker was a tall, thin woman wearing a brightly colored headscarf. She had a long narrow nose, long narrow arms, and a long narrow skirt that almost touched the ground. Walking beside her was Awful Uncle Aleister. He looked, Ben thought, peering through the baler twine and rolls of netting, rather red in the face, as if he wanted to say a lot more in response to the woman than good customer relations would allow.

"Let me take a look at the beast, Lady Hawley-Fawley," he said at last, tapping some ash off the end of his cigar. "I'm sure it's just off its food. These exotic creatures do take a little while to settle in to their new surroundings, you know." He stood there for a moment looking at the dragon apprehensively. Then he put a hand out to it.

The dragon regarded him with considerably more interest than it had previously shown, then bared its teeth—all its teeth, of which there were a lot—and gave a low growl. Uncle Aleister took a swift step away again.

"I want my money back!" the woman demanded crossly. "All fifteen hundred pounds of it, and no argument, my good man."

"If you'd read the small print carefully—" Uncle Aleister started.

"Don't you 'small print' me," said Lady Hawley-Fawley. "I know my rights. Money back, or a brand-new replacement—at once!"

"We . . . er . . . haven't any more in stock at the moment."

Lady Hawley-Fawley put her hands on her hips. "If that's your attitude, then I shall be calling the city council. And the Trades Descriptions people. And the ombudsman. And my lawyer."

And when Uncle Aleister still had nothing to say for himself, she added, fixing him with an uncompromising glare, "And the police!"

"All right, all right. I'll get you a new one."

"And dispose of this one—I don't want it cluttering up my garden anymore, and I certainly don't want the damned thing dropping dead. I can't imagine what the SPCA would have to say about that."

Uncle Aleister nodded tiredly.

"And you can remove yourself and your mad family, too. Famous shoe collection, indeed—whatever do you take me for!"

Then off she flounced, if it was possible to flounce in a long narrow skirt and a pair of large green galoshes, leaving Awful Uncle Aleister (apparently) alone with the dragon.

"Now, then," he said, wiping a trickle of sweat off his forehead. "Just come with me, there's a good dragon."

The dragon didn't even look at him. Instead it nosed at the ground where Ben's dinner had been in a questing sort of way. It licked at a bit of grass. Uncle Aleister took a step closer, then another, and another. He put his hand on the beast's neck. A tiny puff of smoke emerged from one of its nostrils.

Looking alarmed, Uncle Aleister dropped his cigar. "Now, now, no need for that," he said hastily. "Just

stay here, there's a good fellow, while I fetch the car."
And dashed off through the orchard.

Ben waited until he had gone, then emerged from
his hiding place. "You're coming home with us," he said
gleefully.

"Home?" said the dragon. "There is no home for me
in this world." It looked at Ben. "I miss my home. And
I fear I shall never see it again. They will take me to some
other terrible place and either they will kill me because
they cannot profit from me, or I shall die from lack of
care. Or from the sorrow of never seeing my wife and
kits again."

A single fat tear gathered at the corner of one of its
purple eyes and spilled out onto its cheek. Ben had had
no idea a dragon could cry. He had heard about crocodile tears, which he knew were tears cried for effect
rather than genuine feeling, to trick the unwary into
trust so that they could be snapped up by those long
jaws. The dragon did look more like a crocodile than any
other creature he could think of, but it seemed so sincere
and so mournful that he felt his own eyes well up.

Quickly he made a decision. "Right, then. We must
get you back to your home. We must get you back to
Eidolon."

The dragon blinked. "You know my home?"

"I've never been there," Ben admitted. "But I do know a way in." For now he had a plan. And the real beauty of it was that Awful Uncle Aleister would help with it without even realizing he was doing so.

It took twenty long minutes for Uncle Aleister to maneuver the dragon through the back doors of the Range Rover, for the smell of the exhaust, the oil, and the fuel made the poor beast faint with terror. He undid the rope from the post and hauled on its collar. That didn't work. He put his shoulder against its haunch and shoved, and that didn't work either. Eventually, more to get rid of its tormentor than for any other reason, the dragon bolted into the back of the vehicle and crouched there, its sides heaving, its purple eyes watching balefully as Uncle Aleister picked himself up out of the dust, swearing at the state of his suit. But at last it lay down and allowed the man to cover it with a plaid blanket, so that it looked as innocuous as a pile of rubbish.

Ben watched the vehicle meander off along the path, its back end weighted down in a rather alarming fashion, and then took to his heels. He ran through the orchard, past the ornamental fishponds, through the knot garden, and arrived in front of the house just in time to see the Range Rover appear from the road that curled around the back of Lady Hawley-Fawley's estate. Aunt Sybil, Cousin Cynthia, and Ellie were already waiting there. They did not look very happy.

"What an embarrassment!" Aunt Sybil scolded as soon as she set eyes on Ben. "I have never been so mortified in all my life."

"There wasn't any shoe collection, Benny-Boy," Cynthia jeered, digging her fingers painfully into his arm.

"Ow," said Ben.

"Leave him alone," said Ellie. "He's *my* brother, not yours. Only I'm allowed to claw him." Secretly, she had quite enjoyed the scene between Lady Hawley-Fawley and their awful aunt.

Cousin Cynthia was so surprised that she got into the back of the Range Rover without another word.

It was odd being in league with Uncle Aleister, even if his uncle did not know they shared a secret. When the dragon shifted suddenly as they rounded a sharp bend, the Range Rover veered and Aunt Sybil berated her husband for his poor driving, which caused a row and made Ben smile to himself. When the dragon let out a great huff of a sigh, Ben pretended it had been him, so that everyone gave him odd looks, even Uncle Aleister in the rearview mirror. On the motorway, they hugged the inside lane and even the slowest and most battered old jalopies overtook them. At last, when they were overtaken by an ancient three-wheeler, Aunt Sybil could stand it no longer.

"I don't know what on earth's the matter with you!" she cried. "You're driving like an old woman. Pull over and let me drive at once."

There was no point in arguing with Aunt Sybil when she got the bit between her teeth. At the next service station, they switched over and she drove them back onto the motorway.

Soon she had her foot flat to the floor, but still the Range Rover laboured under the unaccustomed weight. "Well!" Aunt Sybil burst out at last. "There's obviously something wrong with this vehicle. I think it must have blown its turbo. It's so *sluggish*!"

Ben had little idea of what she meant by "blowing its turbo," but he loved the description of the car being sluggish. He was tempted to look out of the back window to see if they were leaving a glistening silver trail behind them, a trail that marked his progress into a world of magic.

## Chapter Eleven

# Xarkanadûshak

Ellie, Cynthia, and Aunt Sybil were arguing about the relative merits of Versace, Oscar de la Renta, and Christian Lacroix in the kitchen. To Ben, who had no idea what they were talking about, the names sounded like those of foreign soccer players; but knowing Ellie's absolute scorn for all sport, he realized that was unlikely. When the discussion got heated, Ben slipped out of the back door and into the rhododendrons so that he could spy on what Uncle Aleister was doing with the dragon. He didn't have to wait long before his uncle came out to the garage, unlocked the back door of the Range Rover, and unceremoniously dragged the dragon down the path to what Aunt Sybil referred to as her "gazebo," but that looked to Ben distinctly like a very ordinary garden shed.

"And don't even think of trying to burn it down!" Uncle Aleister warned the dragon menacingly as soon as he'd got it in there. "If you so much as scorch this place, you'll be dogmeat, I promise you."

He stepped smartly out of the shed and banged the door shut. "In fact," he added, through the slats, "that's probably the best plan. I bet Dodds can get a pretty penny out of some of those Doberman owners for a nice dragon steak or two."

"Dobermans," came the dragon's voice. "I used to eat them for breakfast."

Uncle Aleister laughed cruelly. "I doubt you could manage a Chihuahua in your current state." Then, still laughing to himself, he stumbled back up the dark path to the house.

Ben watched him disappear. Then he tiptoed to the shed, unlatched the door, and peered in. The dragon was curled up on the floor with its head on its front paws. It was shivering.

"Are you cold?" Ben asked softly, creeping inside.

The dragon lifted its head. In the darkness, its eyes glittered like jewels. "Dogmeat," it snuffled. "He wants to feed me to dogs."

"I'm sure he didn't mean it," was Ben's automatic response. Except that knowing Awful Uncle Aleister, he probably did, especially if there was any money to be made out of it. Then he suddenly realized the significance of what he had just witnessed.

"He could hear what you said—you talked to each other!"

"Oh, yes," said the dragon sarcastically. "We're close friends, despite all appearances to the contrary."

"No, I mean I thought it was only me."

"Oh, he can hear you, too, can he?" said the dragon. "Wonderful. Good for you."

"No, no," Ben whispered. "I mean, I thought it was *only* me who could hear the creatures of Eidolon talking. But if Uncle Aleister can hear you as well . . ."

"They're all in on it, all those traitors," the dragon said heavily. "Him, the Dodman, and their allies. They always wanted the power your world offered. We should have stopped them while we had the chance, but we never realized how ambitious they were."

Ben frowned. "Who's the Dodman?"

The dragon gave him a hard stare. Even in the night shadows of the shed, Ben could feel its gaze upon him. "Are you deliberately trying to aggravate me?"

Ben felt himself blush. He was glad it was dark. "Mr. Dodds?" he hazarded.

"Oh, that's what you call him here, is it?"

"Why do you call him the Dodman?"

The dragon closed its eyes. "Just pray you never find that out. Now you'd better leave me alone. If they find you talking to me, they'll turn *you* into dogmeat too."

Ben shuddered. "I'm not going to let them do that," he said firmly. "To either of us." He got up and moved to the door. "I'll be back later," he promised. "To help you get home."

The dragon opened one eye and looked at Ben disbelievingly. "What chance does a boy like you stand against them? It's too big for you, all this. You'd best save yourself and forget about me."

"My name's Ben," said Ben, taking a deep breath. "Benjamin Christopher Arnold. And I mean what I say."

The dragon opened its other eye.

"Well, that was brave of you, giving your true name to a dragon," it said after a while. "Thank you. It's a comfort to me to have found one friend in this terrible place, Ben. Even if you're the last friend I ever make." It laid its head down on its claws again in a defeated manner and closed its eyes.

"So that's it, then, is it?" Ben said, feeling sudden anger. "You're just going to give up, are you? Without even bothering to tell me your name?"

The dragon sighed. "What's the point? You wouldn't be able to pronounce it anyway."

"Try me," Ben said defiantly.

"Can I trust you?" The dragon fixed him with its extraordinary eyes, which seemed to spin and spark until Ben felt as if he might faint. Then the dragon sighed. "It seems I must, for you are one of her own. But so young . . . All right then, my name is Xarkanadûshak."

"Oh."

In the darkness of the shed, a long row of white teeth glittered briefly. After a moment of suppressed panic Ben realized the dragon was smiling.

"If you must, you can call me Zark."

"Zark," Ben echoed. He reached out and touched the dragon's head, very slowly. The scales there felt dry and cool under his palm; like snakeskin, but harder. Not knowing what to do then, he gave the dragon a gentle pat, as he might a dog. "I must go now before they miss me, but I'll bring you some food later."

"No cabbage," said Zark.

"No cabbage," Ben promised.

Dinner that night was a salad. Ben picked disconsolately through all the greenery, trying to find something he recognized as food. Both Ellie and Cynthia had declared themselves to be on diets, though both were skinny as rakes, and Aunt Sybil had joined them, since Awful Uncle Aleister had gone out to see a business colleague. Ben suspected it was probably Mr. Dodds—the Dodman.

He went to bed starving. No wonder, he thought as he lay there feeling his stomach complaining, the dragon was so tired and bad-tempered. It had spent several weeks on the Hawley-Fawley Diet: potato peelings and cabbage. He wondered if he might suggest it to Cousin Cynthia.

At last the house fell silent and dark. Uncle

Aleister's Jaguar was still missing from the driveway, but Ben decided he could wait no longer. He crept along the landing, taking care not to tread on the loose floorboard, and slid down the banister rather than using the creaky stairs. Dressed for stealth in a pair of black jeans, a black sweater, and his black fleece, he felt like James Bond.

His first raid was on the fridge. It was a vast silver appliance with double doors, like a wardrobe for food. For a family on a diet, it contained a ludicrous amount of stuff. Ben grabbed a backpack and filled it with a whole roast chicken, two fillet steaks, a slab of boiled ham, some smoked salmon, a big hunk of cheddar cheese, two packs of bacon, a large sloppy bag containing what he suspected to be more kidneys, and a shoulder of lamb. That should do the trick. Then, for good measure, he added a large tub of ice cream and a spoon.

Down the garden path he crept. When he got inside the shed, he found the dragon on its feet, waiting expectantly. It had its head in the backpack before he had even closed the door behind him. Soon the entire contents of the bag were strewn around the shed.

"Mmm," said the dragon appreciatively. "Cow. Pig. Sheep. Fish. Fowl. Excellent: all the major food groups." It nosed at the ice cream carton. "But what's this?"

"Ben and Jerry's Chunky Monkey," Ben said, grabbing the spoon.

The dragon gave him an odd look. "Funny," it said. "It doesn't smell much like monkey to me."

While Zark ate the roast chicken, the steaks, and the joint of lamb, Ben swiftly made his way through the tub of ice cream. Then he helped the dragon open up the packs of bacon, salmon, and kidneys, and watched in awe as it gobbled up the lot.

Ben thought about eating the cheese, then realized that the very idea of eating anything else after all that ice cream made him feel quite ill. He stashed it in his pocket for later. It could be a long night.

At last, Xarkanadûshak had eaten everything other than the backpack. He gave a contented belch and settled down on the floor of the shed with his claws folded over his belly.

"Hey!" said Ben. "You can't go to sleep now."

"Just a little nap," said the dragon, yawning.

"We haven't got time. Uncle Aleister could be back

at any moment. Do you *want* to be turned into dog food?"

All he got in response to this was a snore, followed by another, and another. The whole of the gazebo reverberated with them, as if someone had started up a lawn mower.

Ben grabbed up a garden rake and poked the dragon hard with it. "Wake up!"

Zark growled. Little flames escaped between his teeth, illuminating the inside of the shed.

Ben gasped.

"What?" said the dragon crossly. "What is it now?"

"Your scales. They're . . . glowing."

"That's what they do. When I'm getting ready to roast someone."

Ben backed away. "Well, roast Uncle Aleister, then," he suggested. "Or Mr. Dodds, not me. And if you don't want to go home to Eidolon, then I'm going back to bed."

At the mention of the Secret Country, the dragon's eyes went quite misty. Slowly, he lumbered to his feet. "Come along, then," he said.

Now that the dragon was refueled, making their way the short distance from King Henry Close to

Aldstane Park looked as if it should be less difficult than Ben had envisaged; but he was wrong. First of all, Zark demolished the back gate, because now that he was full of food he was simply too large to fit through it. Then he stopped at the garage and sniffed at the door. "The monster's in there, isn't it?" he asked.

"Monster?"

"The beast they brought me here in."

"Oh, you mean Aunt Sybil's Range Rover?"

The dragon regarded him suspiciously. "That monster, yes. I have a score to settle there."

And before Ben could say anything to stop him, Xarkanadûshak had shoved his head through the garage door and melted all the vehicle's tires. The smell and the smoke were terrible.

"When all's said and done," the dragon said with satisfaction, "they're nothing but cowards, these creatures. Hardly put up any sort of fight at all."

The skin on the back of Ben's neck prickled as if they were being watched, but when he turned around, there was no sign of anyone. "We'd better run," he said nervously, watching the column of black smoke spiraling up into the night sky.

"Run? Dragons don't run, boy; chickens run. Dragons *fly!*"

"That's all very well, but I can't."

"Of course you can," Zark said kindly. "Get aboard." It lowered a glowing red wing to him.

"Really?"

"Really."

Ben climbed onto Xarkanadûshak's back, with the niggling sense that there was something he hadn't thought through. But before he could think what it was, the dragon gathered its powerful rear haunches beneath it and leaped upward with a great whoosh. Ben nearly fell off. He grabbed hold with everything he had—his hands, his knees, his feet. Then he realized what it was he had failed to think about: (a) dragons don't have much for a boy to hold on to, and (b) flying meant being high up in the air.

Ben made the mistake of looking down.

Below—a long way below—he could see King Henry Close receding till each of the huge executive houses looked no bigger than a matchbox. Even so, his eyes were sharp enough to spot Uncle Aleister's Jaguar pulling into the driveway. Their escape had been very narrow indeed. Now the dragon wheeled and soared and the cold wind whistled past Ben's ears. His fleece filled with air and flapped alarmingly. A moment later, the cheese worked its way out of his pocket and plummeted to the ground. Ben had the nasty feeling he might follow, if he couldn't get Zark to land soon. He didn't feel much like James Bond now.

"Down!" he yelled to the dragon. "Go down!"

But Xarkanadûshak was in ecstasy. He hummed to himself as he flew, and as he hummed his scales changed color. In the moonlight, Ben could see them go from red to purple to blue to green, from green to yellow to gold and orange, and back to red again. It was an impressive display; even in his state of rigid fear, Ben recognized that. But it also made them rather visible to anyone who chanced to look skyward at that late hour.

"Zarka . . . Zarkan . . ."

He couldn't remember the dragon's true name.

"Zarnaka . . . Zarkush . . ."

The dragon rolled sideways with a gleeful roar and the air whisked Ben's voice away. Briefly, he saw the tops of trees skimming past and then a surprised-looking owl banking suddenly away from them.

Panic dislodged the word at last.

"Xarkanadûshak!" Ben cried desperately. "We must land in the park. Now!"

At last he had the dragon's attention. It growled, and a little red fire escaped its jaws and expired in the darkness. Then, as if defeated by the use of his name, Zark extended his wings and circled Bixbury like a seagull planing on a current of sunny air. Ben edged a little way up Zark's neck and shouted into the prominence on his head he thought might be an ear, "See that lake there, to the left? Land near there."

Folding his wings like a hawk stooping to its prey, Zark headed downward and the ground hurtled toward them at an alarming speed. There were boys who would be shrieking with excitement at such a ride, but Ben was not one of them. He squeezed his eyes tightly shut and held on for dear life. Luckily, dear life stayed with them that night. There came a moment when he felt the dragon pull up swiftly, then a lurch and a thud; and when he opened his eyes, they were on the ground, in Aldstane Park.

"Not a bad landing, considering," Zark mused. "Rather an awkward yaw to the right as we came in on the final approach. Losing all those scales has rather spoiled my aerodynamics; but it was pretty decent all the same, given that I haven't had much practice lately."

Ben slid from the dragon's back, feeling rather weak at the knees. It felt as if the ground were still swaying and swooping beneath his feet.

"I feel like a new dragon," Zark boasted. "The great Xarkanadûshak is alive and well!" He inhaled a huge breath so that his chest swelled out like a sail full of wind. Then he let it all out in a whoosh. Unfortunately, a great sheet of flame came out along with the air; and all of a sudden where there had been a park bench there was nothing but a smoking iron frame and a pile of black ashes.

"Oh, Zark—"

Ben was about to lecture the dragon on the irresponsibility of setting fire to other people's property when he heard a shout. Drawn by the sudden gout of flame in the black of the night, several figures were scaling the park gates.

It was Awful Uncle Aleister, Mr. Dodds, and the goblins.

# Chapter Twelve

## Eidolon

"Zark! Hurry!"

The dragon's head swiveled to regard him. "What is it now?" he demanded in an annoyed fashion.

Ben pointed toward the gates.

"Ha! The Great Xarkanadûshak will roast them all."

"I don't think that's a very good idea," Ben began. Even though he detested Uncle Aleister, when all was said and done he was still his mother's brother.

Zark took a deep breath as if stoking his fire. Then the moon emerged from behind a cloud, illuminating the figures at the gate, and his expression changed from proud bravado to terror.

"The Dodman," he breathed, and all that issued from his mouth this time was the tiniest wisp of smoke.

Ben's heart clenched. "Like it or not, now you must run! Come on, follow me!"

Across the park they fled, boy and dragon, toward the dark bank of bushes, toward the Aldstane. But this time there was no wood-sprite to light the way. Once inside the rhododendrons, Ben was lost. He had a vague memory of where the stone lay, but in the darkness and the confusion he could not immediately find it. Zark blundered behind him, crushing bushes, breaking branches, leaving a swath of devastation in his wake. Looking over his shoulder, Ben could see Mr. Dodds's minions gaining on them, and with an easy path to follow.

The dragon turned too. "Vile goblins!" he roared. "I shall burn them!"

"No!" Ben grabbed his wing, tugging it frantically. "You'll set the whole park alight!"

On they ran, Ben staring to left and right for the little clearing in which the Aldstane stood. He could picture it as clear as day in his mind, but it was, unfortunately, not as clear as day.

The next time he chanced a look over his shoulder, he could make out Awful Uncle Aleister and Mr. Dodds, too, just behind the two goblins, which must surely have been the creatures he saw loading the truck in the driveway.

He picked up a broken pine branch from the ground.

"Zark!" he cried urgently. "Can you be very, very careful and light this, and only this?"

The dragon gave him a hurt look, then breathed very gently on the stick. A moment later, a flower of fire blossomed at its tip. On Ben ran with his torch held high like an Olympic flame-carrier.

Now he had his bearings.

"This way!" he yelled, charging through a particularly dense stand of bushes. Hawthorn brambles snagged his fleece and dragged at the fabric of his jeans. He could hear the dragon behind him, breathing hard. He hoped it wasn't burning its way through.

And then, suddenly, there it was: the Old Stone, the way-marker to Eidolon.

Now that he saw it, the old qualms returned. Did he dare enter the wild road to the Shadow World, from which he might never return, or should he push the dragon through and take his chances in this one? But he did not think he could outrun the goblins, even if he could evade the men; and he dreaded to think what might happen if they caught him. Swallowing his fear, he ran to the back of the stone, to where Ignatius Sorvo Coromandel and his friends had disappeared.

The dragon cannoned into him, almost knocking him down.

"Why have you stopped?" Zark demanded. "They're gaining on us."

"Look." Ben held the burning branch up to the surface of the stone so that the leaping light illuminated the carved letters.

The dragon stared at the stone, then at Ben. "What?"

Ben ran his fingers over the word. "Can't you see? It spells Eidolon."

Xarkanadûshak gave him a withering look. "Do you honestly think dragons can be bothered with such things as reading?"

There were a lot of answers Ben could have

thought of to that, for he loved books and stories, but now was not the time.

"You, boy, stop!"

Ben's head shot up.

It was Mr. Dodds; somehow he had outstripped even the goblins. He stood now at the edge of the clearing, and his face was contorted with fury.

"Where do you think you are going with that dragon?"

Ben felt his heart thumping, but he grasped his courage. "I'm taking him back to Eidolon!" he said defiantly. "Where he belongs."

"He belongs to me," said Mr. Dodds. "And I have all the paperwork to prove it!" He flourished a bundle of documents.

Xarkanadûshak raised his head and roared. A line of red flame lasered the night, and a moment later the papers were fluttering away as tiny black ashes on the breeze, and Mr. Dodds was swearing and holding his injured hand to his chest.

"You'll regret that!" he promised, and it seemed to Ben as if his teeth had grown longer and sharper. "Both of you."

"Quickly, Zark, into the wild road!" Ben urged.

He thrust out his hand and they both watched as it disappeared from view.

The dragon blinked. Then he took a step backward.

"But I don't want to disappear," he said uncertainly.

"It's the only way back to your home!" Ben cried desperately. "It's the only way I know into Eidolon."

By now, Awful Uncle Aleister and the goblins had joined Mr. Dodds. Uncle Aleister was red in the face and puffing like a sick dog. There was a bruise on his head, and several crumbs of what looked suspiciously like cheddar cheese on his jacket.

He stared when he saw Ben, and for a moment he looked afraid. Then he puffed himself up and bellowed, "Benjamin Arnold, go home and go to bed at once! You've no business gallivanting around a park in the middle of the night!"

Mr. Dodds turned to him. "Benjamin Arnold? Your nephew?" He looked from Uncle Aleister to Ben and back again. "*Her* son?"

"Izzy's boy, yes."

Mr. Dodds grimaced so that his teeth shone in the darkness. "I might have known," he hissed. "And

186

indeed, Aleister, you might have told me." He paused. "It is so much easier to have enemies than allies; at least you always know exactly where you stand with them." He fixed his gaze on Ben once more. "You do have a look of her," he said grimly. His eyes narrowed. "But aren't you the boy who bought that blasted cat from me?" he asked suddenly.

Ben nodded uncertainly.

"Damn the meddler!" Dodds howled. "What a mess. We'd better sort this out, Benjamin Arnold, once and for all. Before it gets out of hand." He took a step forward.

Ben pushed the dragon. "Go!" he said urgently. "Go on . . ."

One of the goblins giggled, showing a lot of black teeth, which complemented its long black claws perfectly.

"Let us eat him," the goblins begged Mr. Dodds. "Lovely fresh boy."

"Oh, no," said Mr. Dodds. "I have other plans for him. You will capture him but draw no blood. I know what you are like when you draw blood." He pushed back his suit sleeves and extended hands like claws.

Ben blinked. They *were* claws.

"Get in the wild road, Xarkanadûshak!" he yelled.

Compelled by the use of its true name, the dragon gave Ben an accusatory look, then took a tentative step into the wild road. One foreleg shimmered and disappeared, followed by part of his head. Then, with a bound, the dragon gathered his haunches and sprang, and just like that he was gone.

At the moment when the tip of Zark's scaly tail vanished behind the Aldstane, someone grabbed Ben's arm.

It was one of the goblins, its wicked little teeth bared in a vicious grin. "Got you!"

In a gesture born more of panic than intent, Ben thrust the flaming pine branch into its face. With a shriek, the goblin released its grip, and in that second, Ben threw the torch at the other goblin and dived into the wild road.

All at once he felt as though he had been caught up by a whirlwind and hurled over and over, a tiny speck of life in the grip of something scary and elemental. The world flashed past in a rush of color, a blur of shapes, a flicker of light and shade. The question was: which world?

Perhaps, thought Ben, suddenly afraid, only those who fully belonged to the Secret Country could survive the transition. He would perish, and no one would know. He thought of his mother lying in her hospital bed, hooked up to tubes and monitors, her paper-thin eyelids closed, and bitterly regretted his decision. But even as he pictured her thus, her eyes opened wide. "Oh, Ben," she whispered. "Be brave, be careful. Take heart. . . ."

It was only a dream, a wish; but even so, it made all the difference. Ben gritted his teeth and took heart.

The world stopped spinning.

He took a deep breath and looked around. It was night here and he was in a forest, next to a standing stone that looked very much like the one he had just stepped into. But everything *felt* different. He could not define it, but it was as if he felt more alive, all over. His skin tingled as if an electric current had been passed through him. Was this what magic felt like? Or was he just scared? He turned around and stared into the darkness. Where was the dragon? There was no sign of it at all. He found that even though there was not much moonlight, he could see remarkably well. But only out of one eye. If he closed his green right eye, he found, the world became dim and obscure; but if he closed his brown left eye and looked with his right it came into sharp focus.

How curious.

But Ben did not have time to ponder this oddity, for there came a great din through the air and then he heard the voice of Mr. Dodds, strangely amplified so that it boomed like a bloodhound's baying: "Benjamin Arnold, come to me!"

First Ben thought, *He must be joking!* Then he thought, *He's trying to make me do what he wants by using my true name.* And finally he thought, *Thank goodness he doesn't know it.*

But Mr. Dodds was with his uncle. An icy hand of fear gripped Ben's heart. Did Awful Uncle Aleister know his full name? Given that his uncle tended to address him as Benny, and never Ben or even Benjamin, he rather thought he might not. But he could not simply trust to luck. Head down, using the good eye to spy his way between the tangle of trees and brambles, Ben ran.

He stared uncertainly up into the mysterious darkness, scrutinizing the black, abstract patterns for the sign of any predator, ready to run for his life. His skin prickled. He could *feel* something watching him, as if the magic in this place made him unnaturally alert. Branches, leaves, sky, moon, branches . . . And a pair of eyes!

Ben felt his heart stop, then jump into rapid rhythm. Eyes were watching him: a pair of wide, amber eyes that belonged to something other than an owl.

Terrified, he chanced a glimpse back over his shoulder: Perhaps a safer route through this strange and frightening place lay on the other side of the thicket. But then a shattered rainbow of light bounced off the trees behind him, and for a second, very clearly outlined by that unearthly glow, he saw four figures. The first two were the goblins; the third he could hardly make out at all; but the fourth was so terrifying that he forgot to turn back to see where he was going and tripped and fell headlong, hitting the ground so hard he could not help but cry out.

The next thing he knew, one of the trees had grabbed him.

## Chapter Thirteen

# Captive

Ben struggled, but the tree just held him tighter. *Oh, no,* he thought in despair, *if even the trees are in league with Mr. Dodds, what chance do I have?*

As if in response to Ben's growing panic, one of the tree's branches wrapped itself around his neck, its twigs like fingers holding his mouth closed, while others twined around his ankles and knees until he could not move an inch.

All he could do was stare, wide-eyed, as his pursuers came through the forest in search of him. The goblins ran ahead, their eyes glinting in the gloom. They looked exactly the same as they had before, but the two figures behind them hardly resembled Awful Uncle Aleister or Mr. Dodds at all. The smaller of the two was hunched and bald, his face wizened, his teeth and nails horribly overgrown. He looked, Ben thought, like his uncle might look if he were about three hundred years old, except that he moved with an unsettling vigor. But he had a bruise in exactly the same place as his uncle's, and Ben thought that if he squinted he could see crumbs of cheddar on the shoulder of the robe he wore. Behind him was the figure that had so transfixed Ben: no longer Mr. Dodds in this world, but surely the Dodman himself.

Looming eight feet tall and more, he strode through the undergrowth, looking to left and right. To the shoulder he was a man; but from the neck up he had the head of a great black dog, like an Egyptian god Ben had once seen in a book. Like the figure he had seen in his nightmare.

Ben started to tremble at the sight of his uncle and Mr. Dodds in their shocking new Eidolon forms, which seemed to reflect their inner natures in a most disturbing way. The tree squeezed his ribs so that he could hardly breathe.

As the dog-headed figure walked, he sniffed; with his nose, his mouth open as if he were tasting the air. Moonlight gleamed on twin rows of razor-sharp teeth.

Leaves curled themselves around Ben's face and he felt his legs being encased in bark. It was hard to know which was worse: to be eaten alive by a tree, or to be found by the thing that the dragon had called the Dodman, and the horrible old man who had once been his uncle. Ben closed his eyes.

"I can smell you, Benjamin Arnold!"

And now the Dodman looked in his direction and smiled.

"Nothing can save you, Ben, not in my world."

He stared around, his great, black, doglike eyes silvered by moonlight so that it seemed that they had been replaced by a pair of shiny steel ball bearings. His gaze fixed itself on a point to Ben's right and his ears flicked—once, twice—as if he were listening to something beyond the range of ordinary hearing. Then he walked right up to the tree in which Ben was imprisoned. Ben could feel his hot breath even through the veil of leaves.

"Release him!" he ordered the tree.

Ben felt the tree quiver, as if a great wind had caught it and shaken it to the core; but still it did not let him go. And now that he saw the Dodman up close, towering over him, Ben decided he would rather be absorbed into the tree than taken by such a monster.

Now the Dodman lashed out at the tree with a booted foot and Ben heard it moan, as anyone might who'd been kicked by a bully.

"Let him go!"

"I shan't!"

Ben tensed. The voice—which was light and gentle, and female, and very determined—seemed to have come from above him, and yet all around him, as if the tree itself had spoken. Which was impossible, wasn't it?

"If you do not, it will be the worse for you, Dryad."

*Dryad?* Ben puzzled over this. It was a word he half remembered from his books of mythology.

"Leave him be," said the voice of the tree. "I have offered him the protection of these woods, and if you do not go, it will be the worse for *you!*"

"You do not know this boy, or what he has done, so why would you risk your welfare for him? He is a thief and a renegade," the Dodman growled, "and *you* will give him up to me."

"Elves and wood nymphs have a kinship; and if this young elf is being chased by one such as you, then I know who is more likely to be in the right," the dryad retorted defiantly.

Now things were taking a very odd turn indeed. Talking trees were one thing, but wood nymphs and elves? What was she talking about?

"The boy is only half elven, which lessens your ties commensurately," the Dodman said smoothly. "And he has meddled in things that are not his business. Now, if you will not give him up to me willingly, perhaps a show of force is required." He turned to the old man. "Aleister, I believe a little fire is called for: you have some matches?"

And now Ben felt the tree shiver in a kind of dread.

Clutching what appeared to be an ordinary matchbox in his gnarled hand, the awful old man stepped to the foot of the tree and tried to strike a match. In his own world, Uncle Aleister could light a cigar even in a high wind; but in the Shadow World his horrible long nails got in the way—he fumbled the first match, dropped it on the ground. He managed to strike the second, but almost set fire to his robe. The Dodman looked on, unimpressed. "Give the matches to the goblins!" he hissed, but they shook their heads and backed away.

The Dodman snatched the box from Awful Uncle Aleister's ancient hands. But his fingers were claws, with hard black nails just like a dog's, and they were not made for the delicate task of striking a match.

The Dodman's eyes flashed in frustration; and for a moment Ben thought that, having lost face so, he might just give up and go away. It was a foolish hope. A moment later, the dog-headed man threw back his snout and roared up into the sky, "Xarkanadûshak!"

Ben's heart missed a beat, then fell like a cold stone into his stomach.

On the other side of the clearing, a black shape rose in the sky and beat its wings slowly as if making up its mind whether or not to heed the call, then it wheeled and dived into the dark canopy of the forest. Moments later there came a great snuffling and rustle of undergrowth, and the dragon emerged between the trees. It looked puzzled and ashamed, and when the Dodman turned to it, it shuddered.

"You summoned me," Zark said dully.

"Ah, yes." The Dodman's great black muzzle wrinkled with distaste, and perhaps a little mirth. "I have a job for you. I want you to burn down this tree."

Zark raised his head reluctantly and regarded the ash tree. His eyes narrowed, then gleamed. "I cannot burn a dryad," he said. "She is a sacred creature."

"If you do not, I will bind you to me as my slave for the rest of your days. And I hear dragons' lives are long. . . ."

Xarkanadûshak hung his head.

The tree's hold on Ben slackened minutely as the dryad realized the implications of the Dodman's threat. Taking this chance, Ben thrust his chin free from her branches and shouted, "No!"

Everyone stared at him.

For a moment, Ben felt as if he were two people in one skin: one, a frightened boy lost in a world he did not understand, menaced by creatures beyond imagination; the other, a proud and angry denizen of Eidolon, whose birthright it was to walk the Shadow World freely and without fear.

"Release me, Dryad," he said at last. "I can't allow them to hurt you just to save my own skin; and I can't let my friend Zark, whose true name I so stupidly allowed the Dodman to hear, to be used in such a way."

"But he will hurt you," she said softly, so softly it was like the sound of leaves rustling in a breeze. "He is the Dodman and his companion is Old Creepie. They hate all magical things and are doing everything they can to bring the world to ruin."

"Even so," said Ben, trying to sound brave even though his knees were trembling. "Two wrongs don't make a right." It was another of his mother's sayings. "Thank you, Dryad, for trying to save me, but I don't want to put anyone else in danger. Please let me go."

"Ahhhh . . ." The dryad sighed.

Then, very slowly, the tree released its grip upon him. Vines and bark unfurled from his legs; branches unpeeled themselves from his arms and chest. At last he stood on his own two feet on the forest floor. But even though Ben felt the Dodman's compelling gaze upon him, he could not resist turning to see what a dryad might look like.

At first, all he could see was an ash tree; a tree that looked very similar to the ash that stood on the border of Aldstane Park. Then he closed his left eye and focused with his right, and at once he could discern a shadowy form within the gnarled bark of the tree. As if in response to his interest, the dryad moved, and Ben saw the shape of a lithe, brown-skinned woman within the tree. Her eyes were the bright green of new buds. Tears stood in them like dew. She sighed.

"At first I thought you one of my elves; but even as I held you, I knew you were more. When the Dodman called you half elven, I realized my error," she said. "And now I have let you fall into the hands of our enemy. Your mother will never forgive me."

Ben frowned. "My mother?"

From behind him came a caterwaul of laughter.

"It seemsss the boy knowssss nothing after all! How amusssing!"

Ben whirled around. It was the Sphynx, as he had known it would be, wreathing its skinny body in and out of the Dodman's legs. He had sensed something watching them as he and Zark had escaped from Awful Uncle Aleister's; had sensed eyes on him from up in the trees of the Shadow World as he ran through the forest. The little spy . . .

The Sphynx's eyes shone with amusement.

"You sssee?" The hairless cat said to its master. "He

isss just a ssstupid boy, despite the eyesss and all the trouble he has given usss."

The Dodman grimaced. "I thought you said he knew all about the Shadow World. That he had been talking with that infernal cat."

"The Wanderer? The Wanderer isss an idiot. He did not even recognise hisss own Queen, not even when he wasss in the boy's houssse!"

"But . . . the Wanderer never came into my house," Ben said slowly, trying to piece all this strangeness together. He turned to the dryad again. "Who is my mother?" he asked, his heart pounding. *And who am I?* he wondered.

"Your mother is Queen Isadora," said the dryad. "Long ago, when she was barely more than a girl, she was dancing in these woods—they were different then, you understand, with sunlit glades and ponds full of nymphs, not gloomy and grim as they are now—and she danced a wild road into existence, a way between worlds. The next thing she knew, she was in a different sort of wood entirely, a place where it seemed no magic existed at all. But by some strange chance or fate, a new kind of magic overtook her, for there she met an inhabitant of this other world, and they fell in love. . . ."

"Ah, such a sweet tale." It was the old man who spoke, but his face was at odds with his words, for it was twisted into a grimace. "My stupid sister, falling for that good-for-nothing human lump, Clive Arnold!"

Ben's mouth fell open. Clive Arnold, his father? Now he was very confused. His mother was a queen? He was an elf—or, actually, half elf? And as for dancing wild roads into existence . . . Part of him felt adrift and bemused; but another part of him accepted these strange offerings as facts, facts that began to bring the two parts of himself into clearer focus.

"She should have been mine!" Now it was the Dodman who spoke so bitterly, and a red light flickered in his eyes like little fires. "She is wasting in the Other World now; but she shall be mine, when she is too weak to resist me any longer!"

The dryad regarded the dog-headed man in disgust. "You may steal the magic out of Eidolon; you may disperse it through the wild roads and destroy the delicate balance between the worlds; you may bring Isadora to the brink of death by your cruel trade; but she will never love you!"

The Dodman narrowed his eyes at her. "Love?

Who speaks of love? Love is for weaklings and fools. I shall take her without love, and make her magic mine; and then I will be the Lord of Eidolon."

The dryad laughed, but there was no humor in the sound. "She is stronger than you think, Dodman. Love and its consequences will defeat you in the end. For when Isadora left our world and fell in love with the human man Clive Arnold, she stayed to have his children and thus began to fulfill the ancient prophecy." She turned her luminous green gaze upon Ben. "Ben Arnold, Prince of Eidolon, I am sorry I have failed to save you. Perhaps your mother could forgive me, but I do not think I can forgive myself."

And she buried her face in her hands and wept.

## Chapter Fourteen

# The Castle of the Gabriel Hounds

Then the goblins came cackling toward him carrying two lengths of flexible vine.

"Bind his hands!"

"And his foots!"

"Feet!"

"Foots!"

"Fools!" cried the Dodman. "If you bind his feet, how will he walk?"

The goblins looked at one another.

"Idiot!"

"Numskull!"

"Featherhead!"

"Toad-brain!"

Ben regarded them with his jaw clenched. They had sharp noses and cruel little red eyes that sparkled in the gloom. Was this Darkmere Forest, and were these the goblins Iggy had warned him about, the ones you wouldn't want to meet on a dark night? It *was* dark in the forest, and he fervently wished he had not met them. He wondered how far and how fast he could run if they tried to grab him. At school he had always come second to his friend Adam when they ran the hundred meters, but he could beat Adam if the race was over two hundred meters. Of course, that was on the flat, in the daylight. And in another world.

"Don't even think about trying to get away, Ben Arnold," snarled the creature who had once been his Uncle Aleister, but whom the dryad had called Old Creepie. Old Creepie suited him well, Ben thought, with his sallow skin and his bent back, his big bald head and those horrid long nails and teeth. "Goblins can run much quicker than human boys and as fast as an elf; and since you are only half of one and half of the other, I would not think you have much chance against them."

"Besides," said the Dodman, offering Ben a ghastly grin, "if you try to escape, I will make sure your friend here suffers." And he gave the dragon a look of such malice that Zark began to shake with fear.

Slowly, Ben offered his hands up to the goblins. There was nothing else he could do. The goblins tied the vines with swift expertise, as if they had had a good deal of practice at subduing captives.

It seemed that being an elf, or even a prince, in the Shadow World didn't give him much in the way of special powers or privileges—if any of it was true, and not just a fairy story. Ben shuffled along behind the Dodman and poor Zark, aware of his transformed uncle and the pair of goblins at his heels.

He wanted to talk to the dragon, to ask him questions about this Secret Country; but when he softly called Zark's name, the dog-headed man turned around and glared, and the dragon looked imploringly at Ben and gave him the tiniest shake of the head. It seemed that the Dodman had broken his spirit.

Ben felt very alone. He was anxious, too—anxious about being a captive in the hands of the frightening Dodman, and anxious about being in a world he didn't understand. *Maybe*, he thought to himself, *if I can think about my circumstances as more of an adventure than a trial, I might cope with them better.* And so, determined not to feel too sorry for himself, he started to take in his surroundings, trying to see if he could make that strange shift with his eyes happen again.

It worked.

He found that if he stared at the Shadow World with his left eye it looked slightly out of focus, as if he needed glasses. He saw things in terms of the world he thought of as home: trees and birds and flowers and shifting patterns of light and shade as the sun slipped over the hills and moved higher in the sky.

But when he looked at the same scene with his right eye, he nearly cried out! For now the view took on a far more distinctive and unsettling character. First, the things he had thought were buzzards planing high up among the wispy clouds now looked suspiciously like pterodactyls, dinosaur-birds that had been thought to be extinct in his own world for millions of years. The trees had faces, and one of them winked at him as he passed, while another waved twiggy hands at him and made a silent roar. Some of the flowers *were* flowers, though of strange shapes and colors; but others cast out what looked like tongues and tentacles, as if searching for something tasty to eat. And in the shifting patterns of shadow beneath the trees were other sorts of creatures entirely.

He saw a group of gnomes gathered in the midst of tall, spotted toadstools; but they did not look much like the benevolent plaster gnomes that some people kept in their gardens back home in Bixbury, with their merry belled caps and bright trousers and fishing rods. No, these wore no clothing but long shirts of woven grass, and had eyes as black and glittery as anthracite as they watched him pass.

Indeed, many eyes watched the strange procession—from up in the branches, from stands of giant fern, from burrows in the ground: an elf-boy pulled along by two Darkmere goblins, followed by the Dodman, a dragon, and Old Creepie. At the sight of the dog-headed man, many of those onlookers bolted for safety and watched from a distance, or took wing if they could. They had over the past months become used to seeing creatures leaving the Shadow World, not being brought into it. Only one, a tall figure wearing the antlers of a great stag, watched boldly and did not hide his face.

Ben stared at him, and a little shiver ran down his spine—as if a memory had stirred, somewhere so deep inside him that he could not quite catch hold of it. Surely he had seen him somewhere before? He was about to ask Zark who the antlered man might be when the figure stepped out from the deep cover of the trees and dappled sunlight fell upon him. He wore nothing but oak leaves, Ben saw, and his skin had a greenish cast to it.

"This is my woodland!" he cried, addressing the dog-headed man boldly. "You have not asked my permission to traverse it, Dodman. And you of all folk know that you are not welcome in my domain, alone or in company. I have heard tell that you have been stealing away the creatures of Eidolon and removing them from our world. Is this true?"

He paused as if waiting for a response to this accusation; but the dog-headed man looked away.

"I know that it must be," the antlered one continued, "for I have sensed the balance of nature changing. And I have seen the effects of this theft." He cast his arms wide. "My woods are not as beautiful as once they were and my creatures are afraid. They cower from strangers where once they walked freely and without fear, as is the right of all the folk of Eidolon. I tend my own as well as I am able, but two of my unicorns and a number of my sprites are missing. The goblins have always been a law unto themselves, but it pains me to see a pair of them in your thrall. I hear that in the wider world things are far worse, and yet the Lady has not returned to halt the damage. What have you done with her, Dodman?"

The dog-headed man smiled now, and his teeth glittered in the sunlight. "I? I do not have her," he said, as if in indignation. "Do not blame me for her absence, Horned Man."

The Horned Man stared hard at the Dodman until he looked aside. Ben could feel his captor's anger boiling like the heat from a radiator. And something else, too. Was it a kind of fear?

Now the Horned Man turned his attention to the creature who was, in another world, Ben's uncle. "And you, Old Creepie!" he challenged. "You are her brother. You must know where our Queen is, and why she has not come back to us?"

But the dreadful old man merely showed his horrible slimy teeth and laughed. "Isadora chose to go away. And she's never coming back!" he cried triumphantly.

"No!"

Ben surprised himself by his outburst. Everyone stared at him. He started to say something else, to tell the Horned Man where his mother was, when the Dodman took a step toward him and pulled him into a hot, foul-smelling embrace, stifling Ben's words. "Ha! Ignore the lad," he said fiercely. "He's a simple-minded creature and entirely dim-witted: The nonsense he spouts, you never know what he's going to come out with next!"

"Where is it you are taking the boy, and why have you bound him?" the antlered man demanded.

Now the Dodman lost his temper. He gave a low growl. "Go back to your folk, and do not seek to challenge me. The boy is a thief and must be punished. He has nothing to do with you."

The Horned Man narrowed his eyes. "I'd say he has a look of the Lady about him."

But the Dodman would say no more and, wrestling Ben ahead of him, hurried them past.

Ben could feel the eyes of the Horned Man on the back of his head as they moved away from him. For a brief moment he thought about breaking from the dog-headed man's grasp and fleeing to the antlered man's side; then he remembered that the Dodman held Zark captive, and would probably burn the whole forest to take him back. And so, with all sorts of confusing thoughts charging around his head, he stumbled on, away from the only allies he seemed to have in this world.

They walked through forest for what seemed like hours. When they finally emerged into open land-scape, Ben gasped.

Woodland gave way to rolling green hills, which in turn became a hazy purple moorland. In the far dis-tance a line of majestic mountains rose into the clouds. It was the most beautiful place Ben had ever seen. The colors were brighter than they were in his own world, and the birdsong was louder.

He watched a pair of larks high up in the blue air, dancing and diving, their trilling calls a beautiful, sharp song. But when he closed his left eye to focus on them better, he realized they were not larks at all but some sort of sprite or fairy. He grinned as they chased one another, zigzagging like swifts. It was nice to see that someone in Eidolon was having a good time.

He smiled and chanced a look at Zark, but the dragon had his head down in undisguised gloom.

The sprites darted closer—too close. With a sudden leap and a twist that carried him ten feet or more into the air, the dog-headed man caught one of them and held it, squirming, its legs kicking, its wings flapping uselessly, in his clawed hand. For a moment the Dodman stared at the tiny creature dispassionately; then he looked up and sneered and, never taking his eyes from Ben's face, crushed it in his fist and let it fall to the ground. It lay there motionless, its lovely wings all mashed and broken.

Ben was aghast. He dropped to his knees beside the fairy and scooped it up in his bound hands. But its eyes were closed and its chest unmoving. He stared at the dog-headed man with tears in his eyes. "You killed it!" he cried.

But the Dodman's smile merely widened. "It was no

great loss," he said. "They fetch so little in your world, and die so quickly."

Ben gazed at the dead creature, remembering how he had once held Twig. Above him, the second sprite flew as close as it dared, its movements jerky with shock and distress. At last it gathered its courage and darted swiftly to take hold of its dead companion. Flapping its wings with immense effort, it managed to drag the body of the dead sprite out of Ben's hands and up into the air. Ben watched the tiny figures diminish into the blue, blue sky, then pushed himself to his feet, brushing away on his wrist the tears he would not let the Dodman see. As they walked on, he watched the dog-headed man's wide black back with loathing.

"And so another of the Secret Country's folk has passed from the world and the sum total of magic is diminished," Zark said softly. "This is how the world will fail, Ben—with just such careless cruelty. And if a prince and a dragon dare not prevent the killing of one small fairy, what chance is there for Eidolon?"

He was about to say more, but the Dodman kicked him hard on the leg. "Stop moaning, dragon," he growled. "Your precious home can withstand a little more damage yet."

On they went, and with each step Ben's heart sank further; for although the scenery of the Secret Country continued to amaze him with its beauty, he found that all looked well only when he gazed around with both eyes open; when he used only his right eye it seemed that wherever he looked, something was subtly wrong. The grass they walked on was withered, its tips brown and dry. Mildew had coated the leaves of some of the bushes; briar roses in a hedge bore blooms that were rotting on their stems. Insects buzzed indolently; pungent steam rose from brackish water, and fungus grew in the shade—not the handsome stands of boletus his mother had shown him in the woods at home, nor the fresh white horse-mushrooms they had picked in a field, but spindly, slime-capped toadstools and lurid bracket-fungi, things with waving spores and poisonous-looking spots.

They walked for a while beside a stream in which the water was so clear Ben could see every stone and pebble in its bed. But he also saw the dead fish that swept past in the current, white bellies turned up to the sun. On an outcrop beside a rock pool there sat the hunched shape of a girl, combing the tangles out of her hair with long white fingers.

She turned her head toward them as they passed, and Ben saw that she was not a girl at all, but a crone, and that her eyes were glazed white, just the way a trout's eyes turn when it is cooked. As they approached, she slithered off the rock and into the pool, and Ben thought for a moment that she had a fish's tail instead of legs; but before he could look more closely, she had vanished from sight amongst the rushes and weed.

At last they came to the edge of a great lake. By now, the clouds had drawn across the sky like curtains, shutting out the light. The surface of the water looked dull and smooth and somehow tarnished, like an old pewter tray in the kitchen at home that had belonged to Mr. Arnold's mother.

On the other side of the lake stood what appeared to be a castle of tall white stone, with brave pennants fluttering at its four towers. Ben liked castles; he had lots of books about them, and had visited some with his father: Warwick Castle and Carew Castle, the White Tower of London, the ruins of Restormel in

Cornwall, Carnarvon and Harlech and Stirling. This looked like none of the castles he had seen, yet somehow it looked like all of them at once. It was sort of blurry, as if it were shifting in and out of two worlds at the same time.

He closed his left eye and stopped in his tracks.

With his right eye—the eye he had come to think of as his Eidolon eye—the castle did not look like a pretty place at all. It was solid and grim, black with lichen and stains; and the pennants that he dreamed he had seen at its towers were nothing more than ragged clouds. He shivered. It looked a dark and forbidding place.

As they reached the shore, the Dodman lifted his head and howled, a mournful sound that swept across the lake like the call of a wolf pack. Seconds later the cry was taken up from beyond the walls of the castle and then the sky above the castle began to ripple.

Zark stopped in his tracks, and his haunches quivered with fear.

"What is it?" Ben whispered, but the dragon would not say a word.

Ben looked carefully with his Eidolon eye. There, in the air above the castle walls, something was materializing. He squinted and tried to make it out, but the image was so bizarre it made no sense to him. For a moment it looked as if a team of spectral dogs had leaped over the battlements, drawing with them what appeared to be a sort of cart, and were streaming across the sky between the castle and the shore in a burst of light.

As the apparition came closer, Ben realized that this was exactly what he was seeing. He watched them draw near with a fearful fascination.

"Ghost-dogs," he breathed.

The Dodman laughed. "Ignorant boy. They are the Gabriel Hounds, the curs of the wild hunt, and they answer only to me. I have harnessed them for the first time in history. I am their master."

But it did not seem to Ben as if the ghostly dogs much liked their master, for they arrived snarling and wild-eyed, and when the Dodman stepped into the chariot, their hackles rose and their tails curled down between their shaggy legs.

When it came to Zark's turn to get aboard, he drew back, his nostrils flaring unhappily. "Will you not release me now?" he asked miserably.

"Ah, no," said the dog-headed man. "You know

too much. I think you must come with us."

"If I must come with you, let me fly," the dragon implored.

The Dodman regarded him steadily. "Try to escape and you will regret it—I can force you to my will, as well you know. Land in the courtyard and await us there." He waited until the dragon had soared into the air before adding softly, with his ghastly grin, "And then, my faithful hounds, I shall reward you with some fine dragonmeat!"

"You can't!" Ben was horrified.

"But the dogs must eat, laddie." The Dodman showed Ben his unpleasant teeth. "We all must eat."

Ben watched the distant shape of the dragon circling the castle and descending in a flurry of wingbeats. There must be something he could do to save Zark. As the Gabriel Hounds drew the chariot through the chilly air above the lake, all Ben could think about was his friend, who had been so ill-treated in two worlds. The injustice of it made his eyes sting with tears, and he blinked them away angrily. He would not let these terrible creatures see him cry.

So as soon as the hounds began their descent into the castle's courtyard and he was within earshot of the dragon, he stood up in the chariot and yelled with all his strength, "Xarkanadûshak! Save yourself: Fly away home!"

The dragon regarded him wonderingly with his swirling purple eyes, and for a moment Ben thought the use of Zark's true name was no longer having any effect. Then, just evading the snapping jaws of the Gabriel Hounds, Zark bunched his haunches and leaped skyward, beating his wings with all the power he could muster.

The Dodman watched the dragon go with narrow eyes. "Since I may command the beast only thrice, I shall let him go for now," he said. "It is not a gift to be wasted."

With a painful stab of regret, Ben realized he had used up all his chances to invoke the dragon's true name: first, to make Zark land in Aldstane Park; second, to compel him to enter the wild road; and last, to set him free. Now he was all alone in this terrible place. Literally, it seemed, without a friend in the world.

## Chapter Fifteen

# The Rose Room

As he was marched through the castle by the goblins, Ben looked at his surroundings first with one eye closed, then the other. The goblins' spiky little claws dug into his arms every time he paused to peer through an open door, but he still managed to glimpse the faded grandeur of a bygone age as they passed. Beautiful brocades, splendid carpets, and fabulous tapestries caught his attention, but with his

Eidolon eye he could see that now they were hung with cobwebs, smelled of mildew, and were covered in dust. Many rooms were dark, the shutters closed against the day. Still others were locked shut. Everywhere was deathly silent.

"Where shall we put him?" the Dodman asked the hunched old man who had once been Awful Uncle Aleister.

Old Creepie giggled. "Why not the Rose Room?" he suggested. "It used to be his mother's."

"Perfect." The dog-headed man grinned.

They climbed another flight of stone stairs and the old man produced—out of nowhere, it seemed—a set of rusty keys and opened a door at the top. The goblins pushed Ben inside.

The Dodman's eyes glinted. "Badness knows what we shall feed you on, boy. But I dare say we can find you some giant cockroaches or a basilisk or two." And he slammed the door so hard that its hinges creaked in protest.

Ben heard the key turn in the lock and the footsteps of his captors echoing away down the corridor. Then he set about exploring his prison.

As prisons went, it seemed rather nice. There was

a huge four-poster bed covered with a heavy canopy. There were bookshelves crammed with books. The cupboards were full not just of old clothes but of odd and rather interesting items—feathers and stones and pieces of driftwood—all the things his mother loved to collect in his own world. And the narrow stone windows looked out over the lake.

But it seemed a sad place, emptier than an empty room should be, as if it were in mourning for its previous occupant. What it felt like, Ben decided, was lonely. And no wonder, for it was as if no one in the world came to the castle; no one but the Dodman and his helpers.

*What a waste*, Ben thought, staring out of the window. If he closed both eyes, he could imagine the castle in better days, when his mother had lived here; when it must have been teeming with life. Laughter would have echoed down its hallways, the Princess Isadora and her friends would have played on the stairs, and people—and all manner of wonderful creatures—would have swum in the lake. In the courtyard, which now appeared to be the province of the Gabriel Hounds, since it was scattered with bones, there must have been fruit trees to steal apples and pears from, fountains to splash in, and lots of fishponds—filled with anything but Mongolian Fighting Fish.

Somehow the castle had been reduced to a ghost of itself.

When Iggy had described the Secret Country, Ben had imagined it to be a land stuffed full of wonders, rather as he had once believed the Pet Emporium to be. But now he realized he had been naive. Just as on closer inspection the pet shop had turned out to be a shoddy front for Mr. Dodds's wicked trade in creatures he had no business transporting between worlds, so Eidolon was no longer the glorious haven of magic Ben had expected.

Neglect and greed had diminished it.

Ben thought about the creatures he had encountered from the Shadow World: the Wanderer, the wood-sprite, the selkie, the dragon. Other than Iggy, who seemed able to adapt himself to whichever world he walked in, the others had fallen sick when they left Eidolon and became sicker the longer they were away.

And at the same time the Secret Country itself was suffering. He thought about the mildew and the fungus, the brittle grass, the dingy forest. He thought about the fish floating belly-up in the stream, and about the ancient mermaid with the blank white eyes; about the creatures that had run away and hidden at their approach; about the dryad's tears, and what she had said.

Perhaps if Eidolon had once had a queen and she had gone away, this was what happened, he thought. Her absence enabled the Dodman to do what he liked, for there seemed to be no one to stop him—not even the Horned Man, through whose woodland realm they had passed, who had seemed so regal and imposing. It allowed Awful Uncle Aleister to sell poor Zark as a garden incinerator and to make tons of money from the sale of the Shadow World's creatures, and thus drain the magic out of Eidolon.

He remembered what Zark had said about the death of the fairy: *"And so another of the Secret Country's folk has passed from the world and the sum total of magic is diminished. This is how the world will fail, Ben—with just such careless cruelty. And if a prince and a dragon dare not prevent the killing of one small fairy, what chance is there for Eidolon?"*

Ben knew it was true.

He turned away from the window and sat down

on the bed. His mother's bed. At once a great cloud of dust rose up around him, making him cough. When the dust cleared he thought he could smell her scent, faintly, in the air of the room: a delicate scent, just like rose petals. The loss of her and of his family and his world seemed overwhelming.

*Take heart, Ben.*

The sense of the girl his mother had once been, here, in this room—the shape of her absence—made something fall into place in his mind, like the last piece in a jigsaw puzzle. He realized, suddenly, that everything the dryad had said must be true. His mother *was* the Queen of the Secret Country: and that was why in the other world she had been getting sicker and sicker. The longer she was away from her world and the magic that sustained it, the worse she got. And the worse Eidolon and its creatures fared, too.

But if that was the case, then he was to blame. He and Ellie and Alice. And his father. If it hadn't been for them, she would be in Eidolon, and all would be well.

Ben curled up on the musty old bed and hugged himself miserably. He was the only one who knew the truth and could pass between worlds, other than Mr.

Dodds and Awful Uncle Aleister and the goblins; and he was here, locked in a castle in the middle of a lake, and there was nothing he could do to save his mother, or Eidolon, or its creatures.

Self-pity enveloped him; and darkness began to draw down.

*Nothing to be done . . . No one else who could pass between worlds . . .*

Ben sat bolt upright. "Idiot!" he cried. He laughed. He leaped up from the bed. He danced around the room. He turned a cartwheel and grinned and grinned.

There *was* something he could do. There *was* someone who could make the journey.

Then he sobered. It would be dangerous.

But there was no choice, and so he crossed to the window, leaned out of it, and shouted out into the night: "Ignatius Sorvo Coromandel! Wherever you are, come to me now!"

## Chapter Sixteen

# Ignatius Sorvo Coromandel

Ben waited. He stared out of the window at the darkening lake and waited. He sat on the bed and dangled his feet and waited. He paced around the room, listlessly opening and shutting cupboard doors, and waited.

There was no sign of Iggy at all.

Then he cursed himself for his stupidity. Even if Ignatius Sorvo Coromandel had heard his call, how would he find him? And even if he did find him, how would he cross a lake? It would be nearly impossible, especially for a cat like the Wanderer, whom Ben knew in his heart to be a rather inept sort of explorer. By now Iggy could be anywhere: He could have taken the wrong wild road and ended up in ancient China; he could be scaring the wits out of the Emperor Napoleon on the eve of Waterloo; he could be stuck on top of Ayres Rock in the middle of the Australian Outback.

Or he could have been dragged here unwillingly and set upon by the Gabriel Hounds.

Ben put his head in his hands.

Footsteps sounded on the stairs.

Ben stared at the door as if by sheer force of will he could employ X-ray vision and see exactly who was out there. The next thing he knew, someone was fitting a key into the lock and the door was creaking open.

It was Old Creepie and the goblins. One of the goblins carried in a plate, the other a mug and a lit candle. Ben's stomach rumbled; but when he scanned the contents of the plate, he realized the Dodman had not been joking.

"Eat up, Benny-boy! Very nutritious, these giant Malaccan cockroaches. Bit crunchy, but I'm sure you'll get used to them," Old Creepie chortled. "You'll have to: It's all there is in this dump. I'll be off home later for a nice steak and chips; but don't worry, Boggart and Bogie will take care of you—make sure you don't try to escape or anything silly like that."

Ben stared at the wizened old man, who in another world was his awful uncle; at his unblinking black eyes and his overgrown teeth, his whiskery chin and sharp beak of a nose. It was hard to see the family resemblance, but even so, he couldn't help saying, "But if you're her brother, how can you bear to let her die?"

Old Creepie wheezed with laughter. "Haven't you worked it out yet, Benny-boy?" He looked over his shoulder in case anyone was listening, then leaned in toward Ben and lowered his voice. "When Isadora is dead, I will bring my Cynthia here to take her rightful place as the Queen of Eidolon."

Awful Cousin Cynthia, Queen of Eidolon? There would be no hope for this world if that ever happened.

At the sight of Ben's horrified face, the old man

rubbed his hands together in glee and gave the horrible, braying laugh Ben hated so much.

Now the old man was addressing his henchmen. "I want you downstairs in two shakes of a salamander's tail," he said, employing exactly the same officious tone he used with Ben and Ellie when telling them to do some unpleasant chore around the house. "We have to go and trap a replacement for Lady Hawley-Fawley's garden incinerator. Just give the boy his meal and make sure he eats it, then join me in the courtyard."

Then he turned on his heel and left the room, banging the door behind him.

The goblins leered at Ben with their little shiny eyes. They put the plate and mug down on the chest at the foot of the bed and stood there looking down at them rather enviously.

"What's in there?" Ben asked, pointing at the mug.

The goblins looked at each other.

"You tell him, Bogie," said the one on the right.

"No, you tell him."

"You!"

"No, you!"

"Rats' blood," said Boggart at last. "Lovely rats' blood."

Ben felt his stomach heave. "You can have it if you like," he said, more kindly than he felt.

The goblins licked their lips with slithery black tongues.

"We couldn't!"

"You could."

"No, we couldn't. The Dodman would skin us."

"I won't tell him," said Ben.

"You will."

"I won't."

This was all becoming tedious; Ben felt as if he had somehow landed onstage in a rather bad pantomime. All it needed now was for someone to yell, "He's behind you!" and the scene would be complete.

As Boggart reached for the mug, Bogie's eyes went wide and round.

"He's behind you!" he hissed.

Boggart snatched his hand away as if burned.

The Dodman was in the doorway.

"Tell me what?"

"Nothing," said Boggart.

"Nothing," said Bogie.

They watched Ben warily.

"Tell you that my mother will punish you for

what you have done to her creatures," Ben said.

The goblins exchanged terrified glances and ran away before the dog-headed man could lose his temper.

The Dodman shrugged. "Soon, she will not be strong enough to punish me for anything," he said cruelly. Then he smiled. "I brought a companion for you," he said.

He reached beneath his long black coat and brought out a dripping, struggling shape. For a moment Ben was not sure what he was looking at; then he realized it was a cat.

"Oh, Iggy," he said miserably.

The cat wrenched itself from the Dodman's grasp and fled, sleek as a rat, under the bed and sat there shivering, a pair of eyes in the dark.

The Dodman laughed. "The Wanderer and the Prince of Eidolon. What a heroic picture you make. If this is the sum of the resistance that stands against me, I have little to fear. Another consignment of Isadora's creatures shipped into the Other World should break her forever. Then I shall take the throne!"

Ben thought fast. He remembered what Old Creepie had said about his awful cousin. Perhaps it was time to sow some discord between the Dodman and his henchman. "But Uncle Aleister said that Cynthia would be the Queen," he said, and watched in satisfaction as the Dodman's head swung around dangerously, his eyes glittering in the candlelight.

"Did he now? Did he indeed? How very . . . interesting."

Without another word, he turned and left. Ben heard the key grate in the lock; then there was silence.

Ignatius Sorvo Coromandel emerged from his shelter looking like a waterlogged squirrel. Draggles of water followed him, puddling on the floor. Iggy set to licking himself dry with surprising energy.

"I'm sorry I brought you here, Iggy."

"I should hope you are. I was having a thoroughly pleasant time watching the sun set on the Western Sea with a very pretty six-toed Jamaican cat it had taken me three days' solid work to get close to, when your summons came through loud and clear and I was off and running for the nearest wild road and no time even to say good-bye." He gave Ben a dark look. "If she won't speak to me when I get back, it'll be all your fault. And if that wasn't bad enough, then I had to swim a lake and deal with a pack of sky-yelpers. For ghost-dogs, they have remarkably sharp teeth." He turned so that Ben could see his tail, the end of which looked bent out of shape. "If it hadn't been for that last one, I'd have been free and clear; but their noise alerted the Dodman. . . ."

"I didn't know cats could swim."

Iggy gave him a narrow-eyed look. "Only Turkish Van cats and tigers do so by *choice*," he said. "Water is cold and wet and it ruins your fur. But I should imagine I'm still a better swimmer than you are, Ben Arnold."

Ben grinned. "That wouldn't be difficult: I swim like a brick!"

Iggy shook himself with sudden vigor. "Right, then," he said. "Better make it all worthwhile and start saving the world, hadn't we?" He regarded the dinner the goblins had brought with an acquisitive eye. "Do those belong to you?" he asked as nonchalantly as he could manage.

Ben looked from Iggy to the plate of cockroaches and back to the cat again. The expression on his face spoke volumes.

"They're all yours," Ben said, and had to look away as Iggy dispatched them swiftly, crunching cheerfully through the lot.

• • •

"Have you got it now? You know what to say?"

"Who's going to listen to a talking cat?"

"I did."

Ignatius Sorvo Coromandel winked. "True."

"You're the only chance we have of saving Eidolon and my mother. Just make sure that Awful Uncle Aleister, and Aunt Sybil, and Awful Cousin Cynthia and her awful hairless cat are out of earshot."

"A hairless cat, you say?"

Now Ben remembered something. "He said he was a Sphynx, and I think he's the Dodman's spy. He did seem to know you. . . ."

"Indeed." Iggy's eyes sparked topaz fire. "I have a score to settle there."

But if Ben was hoping for a story, the cat was disinclined to indulge him.

"Best be off, then," Ignatius Sorvo Coromandel said, giving himself a final shake; though why he should bother when he was going to have to get so wet again, Ben could not understand.

"Be careful, won't you, Iggy? Don't drown or . . . anything."

The little cat showed his teeth. "It really wasn't what I had in mind."

Ben looked around the room: at the locked door, at the leaping shadows made by the candle, at the night beyond the windows. "But how are you going to get out?"

By way of response, Iggy leaped elegantly onto the nearest sill and meowed something scratchy and strange into the darkness.

For a time there was no sound at all. Ben found that he was holding his breath, and the cat sat on the sill staring out into the night as if he were a stone carving.

Then a faint orange glow showed in the air and reflected in the still waters of the lake below it. Ben ran to the window and stared out, nearly knocking Iggy off his perch in his excitement.

What looked like a cloud of fireflies was making its way across the lake. Moonlight shimmered off a storm of diaphanous wings, silvered heads, and antennae.

At last one of the creatures broke from the pack and came flitting into the room, where the candlelight made a golden haze of its busy wings.

"Hello, Ben . . . hello, Iggy!" came a familiar,

scratchy voice. The tiny face was split by an enormous, sharp-toothed grin.

"Twig!" Ben cried in delight.

"And, see: He has brought his entire family," Iggy said proudly. He looked down at his portly stomach, now full of chewed Malaccan cockroach, then back at the approaching wood-sprites. "I hope there are enough of them," he added nervously.

The wood-sprites darted through the window one by one until the whole of the Rose Room was aglow with them. Between them, they carried a tangle of vines.

"We thought you might make a basket," Twig said hopefully. "To put the Wanderer in . . . so we share his weight." He looked at the cat dubiously. "Though he seems . . . larger than I remember." He shook his head sadly. "I was not well then."

Ben stared at the vines. Basket-weaving had never been at the top of his list of accomplishments. Or even close to the top. In fact, if forced to admit to it, he had not the faintest idea how to set about such a task. And yet the Wanderer's fate depended on this. He took the vines from the sprites and sat down on the bed with them.

Half an hour came and went, and all Ben had to show for his efforts was a lot of broken bits of leaf and vine and a worse tangle than there had been before. He grimaced. "Er, this isn't going well, Iggy."

The cat gave him a hard, flat-lidded look. "I realized that a long time ago." He wandered off across the room, dug a claw into the first wardrobe he came to, and casually flicked it open.

Inside was a jumble of dresses and shawls, capes and hats. Ben leaped to his feet, scattering vine everywhere, and ran over to root through it all. At last he emerged triumphant with a frilly, wide-brimmed, lace-trimmed bonnet. "There you go!" he declared. "Perfect!"

Iggy eyed the bonnet with distaste. "I wouldn't be seen dead in it."

"You're not going to wear it, stupid," Ben said impolitely. "You're going to sit in it, and Twig and his family will carry you."

"I'll look ridiculous."

Ben put his hands on his hips—a gesture of his father's when he was mildly annoyed about something, a gesture he had not even known he had inherited. "Does that really matter?"

The cat took one more look at the lacy monstrosity, then shrugged. "I suppose not." He paused. "But you'd better not tell a soul." He thought about this for a moment. "If those Gabriel Hounds see me, I'll never live it down. The Wanderer in a bonnet. I ask you . . ."

It made a very odd sight, Ignatius Sorvo Coromandel carried across the surface of the black lake in a white lace bonnet, by a dozen (rather struggling) wood-sprites. For a moment, Ben wanted to laugh. Then he found that he felt more like crying and had to bite his lip. For his part, Iggy stared straight ahead, like an admiral at the bow of his ship, and tried to look as dignified as he could. Ben watched the strange progress until it disappeared from sight on what appeared to be the other side of the water.

Then he went and lay down on his mother's bed and hoped with all his might that the Wanderer's mission would succeed.

## Chapter Seventeen

# The Messenger

Aldstane Park was as silent as the grave as one small black and brown cat with shiny gold eyes emerged from the rhododendrons into the dew-beaded grass of a very early morning. In this world, the sun was not quite up and the dawn chorus was just beginning to stir.

Ignatius Sorvo Coromandel regarded with passing interest a sleepy blackbird on a low branch of the great ash tree, then forced his mind back to the job at hand. (Or paw.)

Ben had done his best to explain where King Henry Close was, but Iggy found that his mind tended to go all vague and hazy when anyone tried to give him instructions: he preferred to trust his instincts. And his luck.

So he trotted smartly along the road, looking to left and right, and tried to remember what Ben had told him about Uncle Aleister's house. Something about a shiny, big, black Jaguar that sat outside on the driveway . . .

After quartering the residential streets of Bixbury for the best part of two hours Ignatius Sorvo Coromandel had very little to show for his efforts, other than four very sore feet. Nowhere had he spied a Jaguar; or any kind of great cat at all. There had not even been a whiff of one. And he was well and truly lost.

He jumped up onto a brick wall and licked his paws sadly. So much for being the son of Eidolon's two greatest explorers. So much for being the famous Wanderer. He would fail Ben; he would fail Queen Isadora; and he would fail Eidolon—all because he could not find the right house. He hung his head.

"Get off my wall!"

His head jolted up. On the lawn below him, a large marmalade cat was watching him with furious yellow eyes and much of its fur sticking out in spikes.

"Off, I said. Now!"

Iggy stared at the other cat. "You might say please," he started, in a rather aggrieved fashion.

It was not a good idea. Before he knew it, the marmalade cat had leaped up onto the wall and had most of Iggy's head in its very large mouth. He felt its teeth digging into the top of his scalp.

"Ow! Let go!"

The orange cat said something indistinguishable (mainly because its mouth was full) and then batted him with one of its paws. They fell squalling onto the lawn, where Iggy managed to extricate himself for long enough to say, "My name is the Wanderer, and I need your help!"

His aggressor removed his teeth slowly, as if he could do so one by one, from Iggy's skull. Then he backed away and stared at the small black and brown cat in an unfriendly fashion, with his ears flat and his nose wrinkled.

"I've heard of you," he said. "How do I know you are who you say you are?"

"Would one cat lie to another?" Iggy questioned poignantly.

Then he said, "I'm looking for a girl called Ellie. She is staying in a house where a big black Jaguar lives outside. But I have searched everywhere and haven't even sniffed one. Nor even a lion or a tiger or a lynx . . ."

The marmalade cat howled with laughter. He regarded the Wanderer with derision. "What great cat worthy of the name would sit quietly outside a human's house? It's a car, you idiot—a Jaguar, a sort of car! You must come from another world if you don't know *that*!"

Iggy shifted uncomfortably. His insult was dead-on, but no cat likes to seem a fool. "Well, then," he said crossly. "Where do I find this car?"

His antagonist got up off the grass and dusted itself off. "I don't know."

"You don't *know*?" Iggy was enraged. After making himself the butt of the marmalade cat's humor, this was just too much.

"Look around." The other cat gestured to the

roads beyond the garden. "There are cars everywhere. That's the trouble with cars: They move around."

It was true: There were cars everywhere, moving around, and a lot of them were black. By now the streets were busy with them as people made their way to work, entirely oblivious to the fact that two worlds were in jeopardy. Iggy sighed, defeated.

"Don't you have any other information that might help?" the marmalade cat asked more kindly.

Ignatius Sorvo Coromandel racked his small brain. "Well," he said. "The person I'm looking for is living with someone called Awful Uncle Aleister, a girl called Cynthia, and a hairless cat. . . ."

The orange cat looked startled. "A hairless cat?"

"You know it?"

"I do." The marmalade cat was suddenly grim-faced. "If anything is evil in this world, or in yours, it is that Sphynx. If the person you are looking for is anywhere near that creature, you may as well give up now."

"I can't do that."

"I will take you to the end of that road," the orange cat said. "But I will go no closer. Beware the Sphynx, and the people in its house; their cruelty is well known." He dropped his voice and looked over his shoulder as if afraid of being overheard. "They keep animals in boxes and send them off to goodness knows where in trucks. A lot of them simply die in transit. It's said that they sell the bodies for pet food. Food that makes you ill. I won't eat anything that's not out of a can, now." He thought about this for a moment. "Apart from the odd mouse, you know." He shrugged helplessly, gave Iggy a lopsided grin. "Cats will be cats."

The two of them trotted along together in silence for what seemed to Iggy, with his sore feet and impatient nature, a very long time, back the way he'd already traveled that day. Soon the trees of Aldstane Park were visible above the rooftops. He felt even more of a fool than he had before.

At last the marmalade cat stopped beside a tall red object on the corner of a street. "Down there," he said, jerking his chin in the direction he meant. "It's the fourth house along. Be careful, and . . ." he paused, then added urgently, "If anyone asks you who told you how to get here, *don't* tell them."

"That would be hard," Iggy said. "Because you never told me your name."

The orange cat looked taken aback. "It's Tom,"
he said. "Or at least that's what the humans call me."
He tapped the side of his nose. "No real name—can't
have you blurting it out under torture, can we?" And
it laughed as if this was some sort of hearty joke,
jumped over the nearest hedge, and vanished, leaving Iggy staring after him in consternation.

The fourth house in the row had no shiny black
car sitting outside. Instead there was a big yellow
truck with a flashing orange light on top parked in
the driveway, and some men in overalls were hoisting
a rather scorched-looking vehicle onto the back of it.
Iggy sat in the shrubbery and watched with interest.
A thin woman in a smart pink dress was shouting at
them, egged on by the thin girl he had last seen at
Ben's house. She was carrying a thin and hairless cat.

It was Cynthia and the Sphynx.

Iggy shivered as the cat's sharp green eyes scanned
the driveway, and he drew back deeper into the
bushes.

Behind them appeared another girl. She was taller
than Cynthia and had long fair hair caught back in a
loose ponytail to show off a pair of very fancy feather
earrings. He remembered her from the time when she

had stuck her head up into the tree house. Then, she had been wearing a lot of sparkly purple paint on her eyelids; now it looked as if she'd been crying, for the black stuff she wore around her eyes was streaking down her cheeks.

For a moment, Ignatius Sorvo Coromandel's heart clenched.

"Ben wouldn't do such a terrible thing!" Ellie said, as if for the hundredth time. "He just wouldn't."

"If it wasn't him who burned Mum's Range Rover, why has he run away, then?" said Cynthia. "Answer me that."

"I don't know!" Ellie shouted. "I just don't know."

"Well, he'd better not come back," said the woman in the pink suit. "Or Aleister will beat him black and blue. As it is, your father will have to pay for the damage." Aunt Sybil eyed Ellie spitefully. "And on what he earns at that pathetic little local newspaper, it'll take him years. Years!" And she stamped off into the house.

Ellie sat down on the doorstep. "Has anyone told Dad that Ben's missing?" she asked her cousin.

"I doubt it," said Cynthia. "Who'd care?"

At this, the Sphynx stretched in her arms and gave

an evil grin, an expression that seemed much more emphatic without fur getting in the way.

"Nobody," it said quietly, as if to itself; but Ellie stared at it, and then at Cynthia, and when they both stared back enigmatically, she yelled, "I hate you and that rat of yours!" Then she ran down the garden path and out into the road.

Awful Cousin Cynthia and the Sphynx watched her go with identical little half smiles on their faces, then Cynthia turned away, went into the house, and slammed the door.

Iggy emerged from the shrubbery and ran out of the driveway. Ahead, far ahead, Ellie was walking at a determined pace in the direction of the town. "Oh, no," said Iggy. "I don't think I can go any farther on these feet." Even so, he gritted his teeth and ran after her. It took him some moments to catch up to her, though he was going at full speed. When he did, he was so out of breath he could hardly speak. "Ellie," he wheezed.

Ellie stopped. She looked around but, seeing no one there, started walking again, faster than ever.

"Ellie, wait," Iggy pleaded, limping after her.

This time she looked down. When she realized it

was a cat that had addressed her, she looked aghast. "I'm going mad," she said to no one in particular. "I'm as bad as Ben. Or Mum." She stuck her hands in her pockets and kept going.

At the bus stop, she sat on one of the little red plastic seats and stared down the road as if willing a bus to turn up.

Iggy made a last gargantuan effort and scrambled up onto the seat next to her. "Look," he said. "I wouldn't be doing this unless the situation was desperate, and it is."

Ellie's face went pale and panicked. Then she dug in her shoulder bag and took out a pair of earphones, which she stuck swiftly into her ears. A thin, tinny whine punctuated by a dull thudding beat filled the air between them.

Iggy butted her leg; she shoved him away. He dug his claws into her jeans and she got up and aimed a kick at him. From beneath the shelter of the seats he gazed imploringly at her, but she wouldn't look at him. Iggy nearly howled with frustration. "Ellie!" he cried. "Ellie Arnold!"

No reaction.

He took a deep breath and then, without even

realizing he was doing it, dug out of his memory a tiny nugget of information that Ben had given away to him in the tree house, before Ben had known what he was doing, or the power that it carried.

"Eleanor Katherine Arnold! Take those things out of your ears and listen to what I have to say!"

## Chapter Eighteen

# The Message

Three buses came and went as Ignatius Sorvo Coromandel told Eleanor Arnold his tale, and she did not notice any of them, just sat there on the bus seat with her hands pressed to her face and her dramatically black-lined eyes staring over the top at him.

"Poor Mum," she said.

A few seconds later she added, "Poor Ben."

Then she ripped off her earrings and stamped them

underfoot. Little bits of feather floated up into the air, were caught in the hot breeze from a car's exhaust, and danced across the road. Iggy watched them go, puzzled. "Those look like phoenix feathers. . . ."

"Those poor birds," Ellie said at last. "Brought all the way from their home in those horrid, airless boxes only to be killed and plucked. . . . I knew those feathers hadn't come from anything ordinary."

And she told Iggy about the jewelry and accessories that she and Cousin Cynthia had made secretly in Cynthia's den, stolen out of the boxes of unusually colored feathers and fur Uncle Aleister had traded in, which they had sold at school for extra pocket money.

"I didn't think about where they'd come from," she said, stricken. "I didn't really think at all. And you say that each creature my uncle and Mr. Dodds has brought out of Eidolon has made Mum sicker?"

Iggy nodded solemnly.

Ellie stuck out her hand. There was another bus coming along the road. "Get in my bag," she said, as it began to slow down. "Quickly."

Ignatius Sorvo Coromandel regarded her nervously and stayed where he was.

"Come on," she said, grabbing him by the nape of

his neck and stuffing him in alongside her makeup and her CD player. "We're going to the hospital."

Iggy stuck his head out of the top of Eleanor Arnold's bag and looked around. There were a lot of smells in this new place that he did not like at all: smells of illness and death and chemicals. The people they passed in the corridors were too preoccupied to notice a cat peering out of a shoulder bag. Some of them wore white coats or dresses and walked at a fast clip, or wheeled metal tables with sleeping people on top of them; others sat wearing ordinary clothes in lines of chairs and looked mainly worried or sad. The sharp scent of anxiety was everywhere.

At last they reached a room that contained nothing much more than beds. Some had curtains around them. Some had visitors sitting beside them. The one in the farthest corner by the window had a lot of equipment around it, including translucent bags dangling from silver poles with trailing tubes that led to a long shape covered by a yellow blanket. For a moment Iggy thought the bags were the same as the ones he had seen at the Pet Emporium, the sort Mr. Dodds parceled out goldfish in; but no matter how hard he squinted he could see no sign of fish in them at all.

A man sat by the side of the bed and the light from the window fell on his face, illuminating his haggard expression. Iggy ducked down and waited, not sure what to do next.

"Dad," said Ellie, and his head came up sharply.

"Ellie, love, what are you doing here?"

Ellie gave him a quick hug, then firmly drew the curtains around her mother's bed and sat down with her shoulder bag on her lap. Ignatius Sorvo Coromandel's ears popped over the top and the man smiled. He put his hand out to Iggy and let him sniff it. Then he stroked the little cat's head and the place under the chin that all cats like to have rubbed.

"I don't think you're supposed to bring pets in here," Mr. Arnold said softly, in case anyone was listening.

"I'm not a pet," Iggy said crossly, but all Mr. Arnold heard was "Meeeee-oww!"

"He's not a pet," Ellie said. "He's called the Wanderer."

At this, the shape on the bed stirred and murmured. Iggy stared. It was his first sight of the Queen of Eidolon, but he had to admit that she did not look much like a queen of anywhere at the moment. Her face was pale and thin, so that her cheekbones showed like knifeblades beneath lackluster skin. Her hair appeared lank and dull beneath the harsh hospital lighting and her eyelids were papery and bruised-looking.

"Dad," Ellie said, gripping his hand. "I know what's wrong with Mum—"

Mr. Arnold's eyebrows shot upward. He put a finger up to his mouth. "Shh. Don't wake her."

But Mrs. Arnold opened her green, green eyes and looked right up, transfixing him. "Hush, Clive," she whispered. "I'm awake." She pushed herself up a little in the bed. "Hello, Ellie, my brave girl." Then her gaze fell upon the little cat. "Hello," she said softly. "And who are you?"

"I am Ignatius Sorvo Coromandel, son of Polo Horatio Coromandel, and my mother is Finna Sorvo Farwalker," Iggy said, then added quickly, "Your Highness." He bowed his head.

Queen Isadora smiled weakly. "I knew your mother. I fear there must indeed be a tale to tell if . . . you are here." Each word was an effort.

Mr. Arnold stared and stared, unable to believe his

eyes, or ears. Was his wife really talking to a cat, and listening to its mews as if they meant something?

Suddenly Mrs. Arnold grimaced. "It's Ben, isn't it? He's in danger. I felt it, in . . . my sleep." She caught Ellie's arm, and there was sudden strength in her grip. "Tell us. Tell us everything you know."

So Ellie began to tell what she knew: about two worlds—one that was full of magic, and the grayer place they sat in now; about Mr. Dodds's Pet Emporium; about the true nature of Awful Uncle Aleister's import business and how he made money from selling the creatures of the Shadow World to the greedy and the immoral; how the balance of all things was being destroyed; and why Mrs. Arnold—known in Eidolon as Queen Isadora—was getting sick as her subjects failed and died in this world.

Mr. Arnold looked concerned throughout much of this explanation, then he looked appalled. When Ellie finished, he said sadly, "Why didn't you tell me, Izzy? I would have understood. At least, I would have tried to." He paused. "I worried that something like this might happen, that you'd suffer from leaving your home to live with me. But I thought you'd be sad, rather than ill. When you first got sick, I thought at first it must be flu or something, but then it got worse and worse, and I knew it wasn't . . ." He faltered, rubbed his forehead. "It's all my fault! If I hadn't stolen you away from your old life, none of this would have happened."

Tears shone in his wife's eyes, but she didn't seem to have the strength left to say anything.

Ignatius Sorvo Coromandel licked Ellie's hand. "Tell him that if he had not met your mother, then neither you nor Ben nor Alice would have come into the world; and that without you nothing can be put right. Sometimes things have to come to the brink of disaster before people realize how important they are."

And so Eleanor Arnold relayed these words to her father, and then told him the plan that Ben and Iggy had formed to begin to reverse the downward spiral of lost magic and lost lives.

"Yes," said Mrs. Arnold. "Yes . . ."

And then she sank back into the pillows with a sigh and fell once more into a deep sleep, which seemed less troubled than it had before.

## Chapter Nineteen

# The Prophecy

Ben leaned his elbows on the sill of the narrow window and stared out into the unfamiliar world beyond the tower room. It was all he had to look at, and all could do to take his mind off the rumbling of his stomach. He had been stuck in the Rose Room for a whole day now and hadn't had a thing to eat.

What he wouldn't give, he thought, for a dinner of Aunt Sybil's kidneys and cabbage!

But even as he thought about it, he knew he'd actually much rather have a hamburger, or some roast pork, or fish and chips, or even (and this was an indicator of just how hungry he was) a salad. . . . He tried to stop thinking about food at all, but visions of ice cream and chocolate cake and apples and casseroles and scrambled eggs on toast and Christmas pudding and Cornish pasties and all the delicious things his mother had used to make for them before she was ill danced through his imagination until his mouth was watering uncontrollably.

"Pull yourself together, Ben Arnold!" he told himself sternly. "You'll be drooling next."

"You already are."

The voice was tiny, at the limits of his hearing. He wiped his mouth instinctively and turned around just in time to see something scuttle across the room and disappear under the bed. Iggy must have missed a cockroach. He hoped that was the case. Then he hoped that he would never be so starving that he'd actually think about wanting to eat it. It was bad enough that he was hearing voices in his head.

His right ear itched, so he did what his father always told him not to, and stuck a finger in to relieve the irritation. When he took it out again, the voice said, "Such a rude boy." The sound trailed away to nothing; but when Ben put his finger in his other ear, leaving the right one clear, he heard another voice.

"Obviously thinks himself far too grand to speak to the likes of us."

This time it came from the far corner of the room, among the draped cobwebs hanging from the ceiling. Ben stared. He closed one eye, then the other.

"Stop winking at me. It's not polite!"

With his left eye he could see nothing beyond the soft gray shrouds; but with his right eye . . .

It was the biggest spider he had ever seen. And it was talking to him. Ben had never been much of a fan of spiders in the past; particularly the terrible tarantula that Awful Cousin Cynthia had owned, the one that had thrown itself beneath the wheels of Uncle Aleister's Jaguar. He wondered if it was poisonous. It seemed a good idea to be polite.

"Er, good evening," he said nervously. "My name is Ben. Ben Arnold."

"I know that. Do you think I'm a complete ignoramus? You should never judge others by your own standards."

Ben opened his mouth to defend himself, but the spider carried right on.

"What a to-do. No one's disturbed me for years and now in the space of just a few hours I've had boys and cats and goblins and giant Malaccan cockroaches and wood-sprites in my chamber. Not to mention *him.* . . ."

"Him?"

"The dog-man."

"Don't you mean the Dodman?"

The spider fixed him with several of its peculiar eyes in a way that made Ben feel thoroughly disapproved of. "I mean what I say, young man," it said primly. "You should learn to respect your elders. Especially those that have been extinct in your world for millennia!"

Ben stared at it. Extinct? For millennia? Did that mean it was dead—a ghost-spider? It didn't *look* dead: On the contrary, it looked alarmingly alive, and as if it might drop on his head at any moment and suck out his brain.

"Some of us call him the Dodman."

This came from somewhere on the floor. Ben felt as if he were being subjected to a very feeble stereo system.

The cockroach came out from under the bed and stood on the stone floor with a nervous sort of posture that suggested it might at any moment bolt back beneath it again. Ben supposed it was keeping an eye— or several eyes—out for Ignatius Sorvo Coromandel.

"Oh, what do you know?" said the spider in an impatient manner.

"I knew his mother," the cockroach replied, "and his grandmother knew my mother—"

"All right, all right," the spider said crossly.

"Excuse me," said Ben. "Must you talk over me as if I wasn't here?"

"Hark to the boy! Anyone would think he was a prince, the way he goes on," the cockroach mocked, waving its antennae about in what might have been a show of humor.

This made the spider laugh, a high, scritchy sound like the squeak of a finger on a wet windowpane.

"Apparently I *am* a prince," Ben said gloomily. He had never felt less like one.

"Well, of course you are. You look just like your mother when she was young," said the spider. "Except that you're a boy."

"Same hair," said the cockroach.

"Same nose," agreed the spider.

"Same eyes—well, eye—"

"Please stop!" Ben cried. This was all too strange. He went and sat down on the edge of the bed, taking care not to crush the cockroach on his way. Odd to think it was supposed to have been his dinner. He thought suddenly that if people could hear their dinner talking to them in the Other World, there would probably be a lot more vegetarians around.

"Oh, dear," said the spider. "I think we've upset him. No need for that, young man. Chin up, as you people say. We spiders don't tend to use that expression. No chins, you see. . . . So someone has told you about the prophecy, have they?"

Ben gazed curiously up into the webs and noticed how intricately they had been constructed. It must have taken a lot of very precise work. All to trap a few flies. He looked at the spider consideringly. You would have to be careful around a creature like that.

"There was a dryad," he said at last. "In the forest. She called me 'one of the children of the prophecy.' But I still don't really understand what she meant by it."

Now the spider stepped onto the outside of her web and with an elegant move began to rappel down a length of her own silk till she came to the floor. Once there, she detached herself from the thread and raced across the floor, her eight legs a blur of motion. At the cupboard she stopped, edged inside the open door, and disappeared. She was gone for so long that Ben thought what he'd said had offended her; but at last she emerged, dragging something with her.

If Ben had been expecting treasure, he was disappointed to see just a grubby bit of cloth.

"Oh, the sampler. I'd forgotten the sampler," the cockroach said. "Show the boy, then; show the boy."

"Don't hurry me! This thing's heavy, you know." The spider lugged at the piece of material, moving it another fraction of an inch.

"Let me," said Ben. He took it out of the spider's many feet and smoothed it out on his knee. Once it must have been pretty, he thought—though he could not say he was much of a judge of embroidery—and it must have taken an awfully long time to stitch. When he looked at it with his left eye, it appeared to be merely a bit of grubby white cloth, about the size of a handkerchief, into which someone had sewn swirling patterns in different colored wools. But when he looked at it with his right eye, he realized that what he had at first thought to be patterns were in fact letters flowing into and around one another in an ornate script. He turned the material upside down and stared as the words came into focus:

> *Two worlds come together*
> *Two hearts beat as one*
> *When times are at their darkest*
> *Then shall true strength be shown*
> *One plus one is two*
> *And those two shall make three*
> *Three children from two worlds*
> *Will keep Eidolon free*

"What is it?" Ben said into the empty air.

But his heart was thudding, and he knew the answer before the spider said, "That's the prophecy, boy. You are one of the three. Your mother embroidered that when she was hardly older than you. But little did she know it was her own children of whom the prophecy spoke."

"But what part in all this can Alice play?" Ben wondered. It was hard to imagine how Alice could do anything helpful at all.

"Your little sister, is she?" the spider asked.

Ben nodded. "She's only a baby," he explained. "Ellie's my older sister."

The spider and cockroach exchanged significant glances. "What color eyes does the baby Alice have?" the cockroach asked innocently.

Ben had to think about this. Alice slept so much it was hard to think of her with her eyes open. He concentrated.

"Green, I think," he said at last.

"And your sister Ellie?"

That was easy. Ben saw her face coming through the floor of the tree house, covered in shimmery goo and spiky mascara. "Sort of hazely-brown."

"That explains everything," said the cockroach.

Ben frowned. "Not to me, it doesn't."

"Tut!" exclaimed the extinct spider. "Surely everyone knows that elves have green eyes."

"Oh." Suddenly it all made a weird sort of sense: It was his green eye through which he could see Eidolon properly. And he could imagine his mother as a girl, her bright-green eyes fixed upon her sewing, her face a study in concentration. She would be biting her lip just as his mother did when she was absorbed by something complicated. When he lifted the sampler to his nose, he was assailed by the scent of old roses. He closed his eyes and wished with all his heart that he was back at home and that nothing bad was happening, in any world.

And that was when the room flooded with a warm and rosy light.

"Oh, not again," said the spider in an aggrieved tone.

The cockroach ran for cover.

"Hello, Twig," Ben said.

"Got Iggy over lake," the wood-sprite told him excitedly. "Now back for you!"

Ben didn't much like the sound of that. "Um," he started. Unlike Ellie, who got on the bathroom scales several times a day and could tell you to the nearest gram what she weighed, Ben had no idea how heavy he was. What he did know, though, was that he weighed a very great deal more than a cat, even one as greedy as Ignatius Sorvo Coromandel. "I'm not sure you can carry me. . . ."

"Not carry," Twig said impatiently, in a tone that implied that Ben was the stupidest boy in two worlds. "Jump; swim!" And he indicated the window.

"You must be joking!"

"Joking?"

Ben did not think he was up to the task of explaining the concept of jokes to a wood-sprite from another world, so instead he just said, "There's no way I'm doing that!"

"It's the only way out," Twig declared stubbornly.

"I can't swim," Ben said, and then because that wasn't entirely true, added, "or rather, I can't swim a whole lake."

"Someone to help."

Ben gave Twig a disbelieving glance, then crossed to the window.

Down below—a very long way below—the lake lay gleaming and black, like a pool of oil. Ben shivered. Who knew what sort of horrors lay beneath that surface? Probably something like the Loch Ness Monster, or Jaws, or a giant sea serpent, or some other scary prehistoric creature. He shook his head and turned back to the room.

"I don't mean to sound ungrateful or anything, but no."

"Promised Iggy to get you home." The wood-sprite sounded as if it were on the edge of tears (if wood-sprites cried, that is). "Found help. It took a long time, very hard, and now you won't go."

"Ben . . ."

The word seemed to come from a long way off. It broke in the air like a wave breaking on a beach, a lilting trickle of sound.

Ben's breath caught in his throat. He whirled around and leaned out of the window as far as he dared. There was someone—or something—down there in the lake. Moonlight played on its pale head, on the ripples that spread out from its movements. Ben squinted. It looked like a seal. . . .

Or a selkie . . .

A trill of laughter floated up to him, followed by a waving flipper.

"Found her!" cried Twig in triumph. "Thought of plan: Bring friends!"

It was She Who Swims the Silver Path of the Moon.

"Oh, Silver—I never thought I'd see you again!"

"Do you remember how you caught me when I jumped from the great tree, Ben?" she called up.

"Yes . . ." He wasn't sure he liked the direction this was taking.

"I trusted you and you saved me. Well, now you

must trust me. If you jump, I will save you and carry you to the shore."

Now was not the time, Ben thought, to remember that it had been a stroke of luck that had really saved Silver, a branch that had caught her clothing and slowed her fall. Between the castle window and the lake there was nothing to break *his* fall. Nothing at all.

Twig flew up behind Ben, so that all the stonework was edged with his warm light. Ben had read a lot of stories in which the hero stepped through a magic portal: This was exactly what the window looked like now. But he was already in another world, and stepping out was a very scary thought indeed.

"Jump, Ben," the wood-sprite whispered.

"Think of your mother!" called the cockroach.

"Think of Eidolon!" cried the spider.

With his blood beating in his ears, Ben climbed on to the windowsill. Tall and narrow, it fit him like a picture frame. He looked down once more, saw how the selkie beckoned, and closed his eyes. Then, like a sleepwalker in a nightmare, he stepped into the void.

## Chapter Twenty

# Friends

The air rushed past Ben. His hair stood on end.

Just as he was thinking that falling was quite a pleas-ant experience, he crashed feet-first into the lake and the water swallowed him like the monster he had expected to find there. Down he went, heavy as a stone. There was no stopping him. The water, freezing and squeezing, got up his nose; he could not help but open his mouth to cry out, and then the water rushed in there, too.

*I'm going to drown*, Ben thought in panic. *I'm going to drown and my family won't know.*

Then suddenly something stopped his downward progress, something sleek and slippery and strong, and all at once he was borne up and sped along through the water's resistance, until at last his head broke the surface of the lake and there was air to breathe.

He coughed and spluttered. Then he opened his eyes and there was Silver's face, right by his own, and his arms were around her neck. Her big dark eyes blinked at him, and when she smiled her whiskers wriggled. Then she said, "Hold tight!" and they were off again, but this time it was more like flying than swimming. All he had to do was to hold on and the selkie did the rest, splashing with her powerful flippers.

The far side of the lake came closer and closer, and Ben was about to laugh in triumph, when a terrible baying split the night. He turned in dread, just in time to see the Gabriel Hounds come flying down over the battlements toward them.

"Oh, no . . ."

The selkie turned too. He saw her eyes widen,

then she struck out for the shore with even greater determination.

But Ben was unable to tear his eyes away from the spectral hounds, or from the dog-headed man in the chariot they drew. The Dodman's mouth was open in a shout of fury and exhortation as he drove the sky-yelpers onward; moonlight gleamed on his long teeth.

"Hurry, Silver, hurry!" he cried.

But a single selkie was no match for the speed of the Gabriel Hounds. Down they swooped, baying for blood; and Ben remembered that they had not been fed. He laid himself flat against Silver's back.

"Hold your breath, Ben!" Silver cried, and when he did, she dived.

Down they went into the cold blackness, but this time Ben dared to risk a look. With his left eye, all was dark and forbidding; but when he opened his right eye the scene nearly made him shout aloud in wonder. They were swimming through what appeared to be the ruins of an ancient city, for all around them loomed broken towers and abandoned houses like ghosts, lost gardens where fish darted between the skeletons of drowned trees. It made him think of the fish tanks at the Pet Emporium, with their pondweed and ruined plastic arches; but what he had seen there in poor fac-simile was now displayed in the awesome grandeur of the original. For a moment he almost forgot to be afraid.

Above, the rainbow colors of the spectral hounds shot through the surface of the lake. Ben's lungs were bursting. He hoped the selkie would remember she had a human boy on her back, and not some weird sort of fish-beast that didn't mind breathing water. He dug his knees in to remind her of his existence, and up she went, flicking sinuously through the waves, a creature at home in her own element.

Up into the air they came, a little way ahead of the Gabriel Hounds. Ben turned back and found they were almost at the shore. What would Silver do then? He remembered the slow transition she had made from seal to girl, how she had had difficulty walking on her flippers. He could not let the dogs catch the selkie—they would rip her to shreds. . . .

"Silver!" he cried. "I can swim from here. Really I can. Save yourself, dive deep and get away."

But the selkie said nothing. Instead she veered so suddenly sideways that Ben was almost flung from her back. He had a fleeting vision of the leading pair of hounds just a few feet away, then a disorienting view of woodland. He thought he saw something pale move between the trees, but the glimpse was too quick to be sure.

Then Silver the seal barked into the night; and it was met by howls, not from above and behind them where the Gabriel Hounds were snapping at their heels, but from the shore. When Ben looked again he saw four great silver wolves emerging from the wood, and behind them two other, taller figures.

"I must leave you here, Benjamin Arnold!" cried the selkie. "I wish I could come with you, but I cannot. Good-bye, Ben, I will see you again!"

And she rolled sleekly so that Ben found himself fully immersed in the water once more. He flapped his arms. He kicked with his feet. He stuck his head out of the water and splashed and splashed. He tried to remember what his swimming teacher had told him when he kept sinking to the bottom; but somehow swimming at the local leisure center, with its dreamy blue water and neatly designated lanes, did not seem to be very useful preparation for trying to save yourself from a pack of rabid ghost-dogs and their mad master. Even so, he did his best, and a second later one foot struck the lake bed and he knew he was nearly there.

At the same moment, something caught at his fleece top, dragging him backward. He felt hot breath on the back of his neck.

"Do not kill the princeling!" commanded the Dodman. "I need him alive."

And that was when the four giant wolves Ben had glimpsed on the lake's shore hurled themselves into the water. Suddenly he was in the middle of a battle. Snarling muzzles, yellowed canine teeth, rancid breath, and furious growling surrounded him. The Gabriel Hounds roared and snapped. The wolves howled and bit. Ben was sure he was about to be mauled, but moments later there was a whine of pain and the grip on his jacket was released. At once Ben kicked free and, scrambling forward, found that he could stand. A moment later he was running through the shallows, and then he was on dry land.

When he caught his breath, he turned to see that the Gabriel Hounds were drawing back in fear from their adversaries, even though the Dodman stood and screamed at them from the chariot. The wolves stood resolute and unyielding, water sparkling in their shaggy fur. They looked magnificent, not at all like the straggly specimens Ben had seen in captivity at the local zoo.

"Come with us, Ben!" A deep voice thrummed through Ben's rib cage.

It was the Horned Man he had seen on his long and miserable journey to the castle. He stood just beyond the line of trees, his great antlered head limned in moonlight. At his side stood another creature straight out of the books of mythology that Ben loved so much. The top half of this figure was that of a young man, with a proud, fine-boned face and piercing eyes. Black hair fell to his shoulders and sturdy brown chest; but from the waist down he had the body of a powerful horse.

"Oh," Ben breathed in awe. "A centaur!"

"He is Darius," the Horned Man said, "one of the Horse People."

The centaur came forward. He bowed his head to Ben, then knelt on the grass. "It would be an honor to bear the son of Queen Isadora to safety," he said.

Ben did not know quite how to respond to this, but he made a fist of one hand and brought it to his chest, as he had seen a Roman soldier do in a film once, which felt right, somehow.

"Thank you, Darius," he said. "The honor is mine."

Gingerly, Ben climbed onto the centaur's back; and Darius rocked to his feet and turned to follow the Horned Man into the eaves of the wood.

*In the space of just a couple of days*, Ben thought suddenly, *I have flown on a dragon, swum with a selkie, and ridden a centaur.*

If it weren't all so dangerous and urgent, he would have been having the time of his life.

"Let us away before the Dodman can follow," said the Horned Man.

Ben chanced a last glance back over his shoulder, just in time to see the Gabriel Hounds breaking from their traces in a flurry before the four white wolves. Over went the chariot, and into the murky waters of the lake went the Dodman with a great cartwheel of arms and legs and a howl of rage.

Ben laughed in glee.

And then Darius kicked up his heels, and Ben couldn't do anything at all other than concentrate on how not to fall off.

## Chapter Twenty-one

# The Lord of the Wildwood

They emerged from the woodland onto the moors
Ben had crossed as a captive just as the moon rose to
its zenith. The centaur broke into a gallop, and the
Horned Man ran along beside him, eating the ground
away with huge, effortless strides. Their moonshad-
ows stretched away from them, sharp and attenuated,
companions to their flight.

Ben kept looking back over his shoulder.

"I am sure my wolves will hold the Dodman at bay," the Horned One said, and the moonlight glinted in his hazel-green eyes.

"Who *is* the Dodman?" Ben asked, his fists buried hard in the centaur's coarse mane.

"The Dodman, the dog-man, the Dead Man; there are many names for him," the antlered man replied. The leaves he wore rustled as he ran. Ben could not see how they were attached—whether they were some sort of clothing or an integral part of him. "But no one knows his true name, or his origin, which has proved to be unfortunate. For a time, that did not seem important—he was not always so powerful."

"Did he become powerful when my mother went away?" Ben asked in a small voice. He had a nasty feeling this was all his fault; his and Ellie's and Alice's.

The Horned Man nodded. "He hoped to wed her. He and Old Creepie had made some sort of cruel bargain. But fate tricked them, and Isadora escaped their clutches, though she did not know their evil plans. At the time we thought it a boon, but none could have foreseen the consequences."

Ben shivered. Then he wondered what would

have happened if his mother had married Mr. Dodds; would he have been born with a dog's head too? Perhaps he wouldn't have been born at all.

"Won't he punish you for this?"

The Horned Man laughed. "The Dodman does not rule the Wildwood, or ever shall. There are still places I can call my own."

"But if my mother is the Queen of Eidolon, is she not also Queen of the Wildwood?" Ben asked, confused.

"I have seen a thousand queens come and go in Eidolon," the Horned One answered without rancor or boast. "Your mother is Queen of Eidolon and she is also my Queen, and I owe her my love and my allegiance. For her part, she is happy to have a friend who maintains the guardianship of the wild places for her."

"Do you have a name?" Ben asked humbly. "I don't know what to call you, or how to thank you."

At this, the centaur gave a little buck of delight and turned his head to look at Ben. He winked. "The Dodman is not the only one with many names," he said. "You may call him the Horned One; Herne the Hunter; or Cernunnos, Lord of the Wildwood."

This was a bit overwhelming. Ben opted for the one that sounded most like a name. "Thank you for saving me, Cernunnos. But how did you know to come for me?"

The Lord of the Wildwood smiled. "One of the denizens of my forest sought me out. I think you know him: a wood-sprite called Twig. He said you saved him from the Dodman. I believe that one good turn deserves another."

Ben blushed with pleasure. It was something he had often heard his mother say.

Soon they were back in Darkmere Forest, and still there was no sign of pursuit.

They slowed to a walk, by reason of necessity as much as for a rest, for the trees here were dense and their roots treacherous to even the most nimble-footed.

The Horned Man led them through a great thicket of ferns whose curling fronds were weighed down by some form of fungus. He shook his head. "My forest has become darker and wilder than it used to be," he said softly. He brushed his fingers against the mildewed trunk of a hawthorn and lifted his hand to his nose. "And something has sickened it."

"I think," Ben said hesitantly, "that might be because my mother is sick. In the Other World."

Darius turned, and his eyes were wide. "The Lady is not dead, then?"

Ben's fingers tightened in the centaur's mane. "She wasn't when I left. But she was very ill indeed." A terrible dread seized him. What if his mother had died while he had been here? "I must get back," he said hoarsely.

"We have bound ourselves to your return," Cernunnos said solemnly. "You are a child of the prophecy. Our future rests in your hands. Yours and your siblings."

It was hard to imagine Ellie, let alone Alice, contributing much to the saving of Eidolon, Ben thought; but the world had revealed itself as such a strange place in the past few weeks that now he believed anything was possible.

They moved in silence among the trees and Ben stared around, wondering which of them harbored the dryad who had tried so bravely to save him from the Dodman, for he would have liked to see her again before he left her world. But none of his surroundings looked familiar, and Cernunnos did not seem predisposed to make a detour from their route, ploughing resolutely on through the forest.

They were making their way through an area of the forest where the trees were more widely spaced when the Lord of the Wildwood looked up suddenly and frowned. "Stay here," he warned. "Stay still."

Running as fleetly as a deer, he made off between the trees, his eyes searching the canopy as if he were tracking something overhead.

Ben stared upward. In the night sky he glimpsed a moving shape, black against the moon. He waited, holding his breath, all sorts of terrifying scenarios rioting through his imagination.

The centaur pawed the ground impatiently. "It is only a short distance to the Old Stone," Darius said quietly. "Do not worry, Ben, we will get you there." He paused, then added, "Or we will die in the attempt."

A few moments later Cernunnos returned. "It was a fire-drake," he said, "quartering the ground in search of something. Dragons are an ancient and unpredictable breed—it is generally better to avoid them than risk their wrath."

Ben remembered Zark burning the tires off Aunt Sybil's Range Rover. "I rather like dragons," he said softly.

On the edge of the clearing where the Aldstane's wild road had coughed Ben out, the Horned Man stopped and sniffed the air. "I don't like this," he said. "There are goblins about. I can smell them."

"That'll be Bogie and Boggart," Ben said. "They're working for my uncle. Or Old Creepie, or whatever he's called here. I don't think they mean to be as horrid as he makes them. They were going with him to trap another dragon for a customer."

"Customer?" Cernunnos frowned.

"Someone who pays money for something you've got and they want," said Ben.

"Money?"

Ben stared at the Horned Man. "You don't have money in the Secret Country?" He dug in his pocket and brought out a few coins. "We give people these and they give us . . . things instead."

Darius gazed at the coins. "Can you eat them?" he asked dubiously.

"No," said Ben.

The Lord of the Wildwood picked one of them

out of Ben's palm and held it up. It was a fifty-pence piece, newly minted. "It is rather shiny," he said after a while. "I suppose magpies might like such things. Or you could let it catch the light in a stream bed." He thought for a moment. "Though pebbles have prettier colors. What do you do with them, then?"

"Not much, actually. You just collect them, and pass them on."

"And Old Creepie is stealing away our creatures in exchange for such items?"

Ben nodded.

The Lord of the Wildwood's face contorted. "Then this is madness indeed."

"We're trying to stop him, my sister and I," Ben said, hoping that Iggy had reached Ellie and persuaded her to do as he asked. "If we can stop him and Mr. Dodds stealing magic out of Eidolon, Mum might get stronger; and if she gets better, then Eidolon might get better too."

"Queen Isadora must return to her people," the Horned Man said sternly. "Or there will be no Eidolon hereafter."

That silenced Ben. He had not thought things through that far. All he'd ever imagined was his mother getting better, but what would they do—he and his father and his sisters—if she had to leave them forever?

As they approached the entrance to the wild road, he felt suddenly miserable. The Eidolon part of himself was curiously reluctant to leave, even though the magical world was blighted and perilous. He almost wished he did not have to go home and face the awful truth of it all. But he knew that he must.

He slid down from the centaur's back. Then, squaring his shoulders, he touched the great stone that was the counterpart to the stone in Aldstane Park and watched as his hand passed into another dimension.

Above their heads sounded a great flurry of wings.

"Run!" came a voice from above. "He is coming! Go through the wild road now!"

Instead of doing what he was told, Ben stared upward into the night sky.

"Zark!" he cried. "Is that you?"

But there came no response except for a streak of flame, which burst through the air above them. Its fiery light revealed the Dodman, in the restored chariot drawn not only by the Gabriel Hounds, but by the four silver wolves as well. The wolves looked bedraggled and cowed, broken in spirit. Their heads hung down and their tails curled between their legs. Somehow the Dodman had mastered them, brought them to heel, and made them part of his wild hunt.

Cernunnos and Darius exchanged stricken glances, and it was the expression on the face of the Lord of the Wildwood that really made Ben afraid. Matters had taken an unexpected and terrifying turn. If Mr. Dodds could bind the great silver wolves to him, he had greater powers than even the Horned Man had suspected.

"Go, Ben!" Cernunnos cried. "Go through the wild road. We will guard your back!"

But still Ben hesitated. "Please don't put yourselves at risk for me." He remembered the way Xarkanadûshak had been brought low; he could not bear that the same fate should overtake the Lord of the Wildwood and the proud centaur.

"If we do not stand against him now, all will fail," the Horned Man said grimly. "But the Dodman is not yet ready to stand against me, for all that he dares to traduce my wolves. There will be a reckoning, but now is not that time. He puts on a great show of strength, Ben, but he will not fight me. And whatever happens here is not for you to witness. Go back to your world and do what you can there." And he pushed Ben into the wild road with all his might.

## Chapter Twenty-two

# The Aldstane

Tumbling over and over in the strange environs of the way between worlds, Ben felt no relief; nothing but despair. He had left others to fight his battles in the Secret Country, as he had in the Other World, the one he called his home. He had a long way to go if he was to become a hero, if he was to play his part in fulfilling the prophecy to keep Eidolon free.

Then he started to fall, but before he could prepare

for a landing, he hit the ground with a thud that knocked the wind out of him. "Ow!"

He stood up gingerly, dusting off his hands and knees. One of his elbows had caught the Aldstane on the way through and it hurt enormously. Quite why anyone should call that bit the funny bone, he could not imagine. Then some inconsequential bit of his brain reminded him that the armbone was called a humerus. Humerus, humorous. It still wasn't funny.

And it wasn't the time to be thinking about wordplay, for something was going on. Ben stared around. He closed his left eye, then opened it and closed his right: There was no doubt that he was back in his own world, for the view out of either eye was the same. He was in Aldstane Park.

He could hear shouting and the sound of people—or something—running. There was a lot of worrying rustling in the undergrowth. Ben wondered if he had stumbled into something worse than what he had left behind. The next thing he knew, half a dozen goblins burst out of the rhododendrons.

When they saw him, the leading pair drew back.

"It's the boy," said the one he knew as Bogie.

"He's escaped!" cried Boggart.

"The boy?"

"The elf-boy, the Queen's son."

Now the other four drew close together behind Boggart and Bogie.

"He doesn't *look* like an elf," said one.

"He's only a half elf."

"Can we eat the boy half?" asked another.

"Nah," said Bogie. "He'll magic you."

Ben was pretty sure he couldn't magic anyone, but he said, "I magicked the Dodman, and I will magic you out of existence if you come anywhere near me."

"He magicked the Dodman!"

The goblins grew hushed. Then they spoke together in grumbling tones that were too low for Ben to hear, and he realized that whatever special powers he might have had in Eidolon were certainly no longer with him now. Even so, if he showed the slightest sign of fear, they would probably tear him to pieces. He remembered Boggart pleading with Mr. Dodds for a bit of "lovely fresh boy" and promptly pushed it out of his mind before his knees started trembling.

Now one of the goblins stepped forward. "Let us go," it said. "If you let us go through the wild road back to our forest, we won't come back."

"And what about your work for the old man?"

Boggart showed his sharp little teeth and hissed. "We don't want to work for him anymore. Nasty dragon . . ."

Ben looked more closely and saw that the goblin was wounded. In the darkness it was hard to see, but the arm that he clutched to his chest looked burned and withered.

"That will teach you for stealing away the creatures of the Shadow World!" Ben said sternly.

"What does he mean by steal?" Bogie asked, but none of his companions seemed to know—they shrugged and made faces.

"Taking what isn't yours," Ben said, feeling as if they were making him sound like a rather pompous schoolteacher.

They all looked mystified. "But a dragon isn't anyone's," said Boggart; and Ben couldn't think of an answer to that.

"You give me your word that you won't ever again do what Old Creepie asks of you?"

"What word?"

"Oh, this is hopeless. What will you do if I let you go?"

Bogie looked at Boggart. "Eat toadstools?" he suggested.

"Jump in ponds; chase fishes?"

"Tease the minotaur," suggested another.

"No, no, not that—remember what happened last time."

Ben felt dizzy. "Oh, go on then," he said, stepping away from the stone. He wondered what they would find on the other side but decided they were not courageous enough to get involved in any fight.

They approached cautiously, keeping their sly little eyes on Ben all the way.

"Um," he said, as a thought struck him, "just where is Uncle Aleis—Old Creepie, anyway?"

Boggart gazed over Ben's shoulder, his eyes wide. "Behind you!" he said, and leaped into the wild road.

Ben whirled around, expecting to see the horrible crouched old man with the long nails and overgrown teeth; but instead there was Awful Uncle Aleister, in a smart suit and long gabardine overcoat. He looked disheveled, as if he had been in a fight. His tie was askew, his pinstriped shirt was torn, and his nose had bled down onto the collar. He stared at Ben with loathing.

"Get out of my way, you vile nuisance!"

"No," said Ben, trying to sound braver than he felt.

"In which case, I shall just have to take you back with me!" Uncle Aleister declared. "And you won't be escaping this time, I can tell you. This time the Dodman and I will sort you out once and for all!" He laughed. "Come to think of it, it's what we should have done in the first place—the fewer of Isadora's children there are around, the less likely it will be that that ridiculous prophecy can ever come true!" And he advanced upon Ben in a menacing way.

Ben dodged behind the Aldstane. "Don't you come anywhere near me!" he cried.

"Boggart! Bogie! Brimstone! Bosko! Beetle! Batface!"

But none of the goblins were answering Uncle Aleister's call.

Blue lights scythed the air, illuminating the bushes with an eerie pallor; and now Ben could hear sirens.

"It's the police!" he cried.

"I know it's the police, you idiot boy. Why do you think I'm trying to escape to the Shadow World? Now get out of my way!"

But Ben was yelling, "Over here! Over here!"

Awful Uncle Aleister launched himself at his nephew. "You stupid little troublemaker. I'm going to feed you to a Tyrannosaurus rex." He grabbed Ben by the shoulders and shoved him toward the wild road.

"You don't want to go in there," Ben said. "The Horned Man is waiting on the other side. His wolves are there too, and a centaur."

He didn't think it necessary to explain that the wolves were currently harnessed up to the Dodman's chariot.

Uncle Aleister looked fearful. Then he got Ben in a headlock and, fumbling in his pocket, brought out a sharp little knife and dug it into the side of Ben's neck. "One more word," he threatened, "and you'll be dog-meat."

Then he stuck his head into the wild road and listened.

When he emerged again, his head was that of Old Creepie once more, pallid and bald, his brows looming over gleaming, sunken eyes; his yellow teeth all snaggled and fanglike—which gave new meaning to "long in the tooth," Ben thought, watching the illusion gradually fade.

"It seems you have not yet learned to be a liar, Benjamin Arnold," Uncle Aleister said. "Too much of your precious mother's blood in you."

He wrestled Ben into the bushes, backing him up against a tree.

Ben watched as the blue lights got brighter. The sirens sounded very close now; the police must be driving through the park. Car doors banged, then Ben heard running feet come crashing through the undergrowth.

"Over here!" someone shouted. "He went this way!"

Torches flickered through the leaves.

Then a policeman stepped into the clearing beside the Aldstane. Ben wriggled, but his uncle held him tight, and eventually the officer went away. Ben felt the arm holding him relax slightly, so he wrenched his head free and bit the hand that held the knife so hard that Awful Uncle Aleister swore. The knife fell to the ground. Ben gathered a breath to shout for help, but Uncle Aleister clamped a hand tightly over his mouth and nose. Blood dripped onto Ben's face. He couldn't breathe.

Just as he thought he might pass out, his uncle

grunted as if in surprise. A tendril of ivy seemed to have wound itself around his hand and was pulling it away from Ben's face. A moment later Ben found he could breathe, and then that he could move. With a desperate lurch, he dragged himself from Awful Uncle Aleister's grasp. He turned to see if his uncle was coming back at him. He could hardly believe his eyes.

The tree they had been standing against had wrapped itself around Aleister's legs and arms, pinning him to its trunk. Ivy wreathed his head and torso and pinioned his hands to his sides. His awful uncle's eyes bulged with shock and outrage.

Above his head, a second head revealed itself. Ben gasped. It had fine features and delicately waving hair, all of the same color as the tree within whose skin she stood.

"It's you," he said, amazed.

"I failed you in Darkmere Forest, and I knew I must do something to make amends," said the dryad, holding Awful Uncle Aleister so tightly that he squirmed in terror. "If Eidolon is to be saved, then we must all do what we can."

"You came through the wild road, without even knowing what you would find on the other side?"

"I followed you. The Lord of the Wildwood saw me go. I think he was glad you would not be entirely on your own."

Ben was astonished by her courage.

"I will go back, as soon as this miscreant has been dealt with and I know you are safe. The trees here have a little of the Secret Country's magic to them—it must have leaked through the way-between-worlds. I'll be all right, for a time."

She squeezed Ben's uncle so tightly that the air came whooshing out of him and his face started to go purple.

Ben decided that Uncle Aleister deserved the treatment he was receiving, so instead of asking the tree nymph to stop, he grinned and said, "Thank you, Dryad. You are incredibly brave. My mother would be proud of you." Then he cupped his hands around his mouth and yelled, "Police! Over here, over here!"

Seconds later, two uniformed officers came running, handcuffs at the ready.

"Help me!" wheezed Uncle Aleister, now more terrified by the tree than by any other prospect. "Help me—this tree is trying to kill me!"

The policemen exchanged glances. Then the sergeant swung his flashlight beam up into Uncle Aleister's face. "Nutter," he said to his colleague. "Complete nutter." He looked at Ben. "Are you all right, son? Has he harmed you?"

"Not exactly," said Ben, watching out of the corner of one eye as the dryad faded back into the tree, leaving the policemen to extricate Uncle Aleister from the ivy.

"Ben!"

Ben turned around.

"Dad!"

Mr. Arnold came running full tilt into the clearing. "Oh, Ben, you're safe!" He hugged his son as tightly as the dryad had done, until Ben was seriously worried his ribs might crack. "I'm okay, Dad," he croaked at last. "Honest I am."

The two of them watched as the policemen hauled Awful Uncle Aleister out into the open and put the handcuffs on him. He glared at Mr. Arnold over their shoulders as they read him his rights. "Dodds will come for you and your family, Clive," he promised. "And when he does, a little crack on the nose like the one you gave me won't stop him."

"Painful, is it?" Mr. Arnold inquired innocently,

taking in the blood and bruising with some satisfaction.

"I'll press charges against you," snarled Awful Uncle Aleister.

The sergeant regarded him with a raised eyebrow. "Really, sir? I don't recall seeing Mr. Arnold hit you. But we saw you run slap-bang into that tree, didn't we, Tom?"

The other policeman nodded vigorously. "Got to watch where you're going in the dark," he said.

"Thank you for your assistance, Mr. Arnold," the sergeant said. "I'm glad your lad is okay. Can we give you a lift home?"

Ben shook his head. He looked up at his father. "We can walk home, can't we, Dad? After all, we've got a lot to talk about."

Mr. Arnold smiled. "Yes, we have."

They walked to the edge of the rhododendrons and watched the policemen put Uncle Aleister into the back of one of the cars. Then the convoy of vehicles trailed slowly out of the park, their blue lights swirling in the lightening air.

"Walk home?" came a voice out of the darkness. "I don't think we can have *that*."

Ben and his father turned around slowly, in a kind of dread.

Mr. Arnold gasped.

Ben grinned until he thought his face would split.

Above them were two gloriously colored dragons, their wings outstretched as they circled in for a landing.

"Zark!" cried Ben.

"And this is my wife, Ishtar," said Zark.

Ishtar glided to a halt in front of them, her scales a fabulous tapestry of blues and golds and purples, where her husband's were the color of flame.

"Hello again, Ben," she said, and Ben suddenly realized that Ishtar must have been the dragon he had seen on the other side of the wild road, the one he had mistaken for Zark in the gloom and panic of those last moments in Eidolon.

"Hello," he breathed, awed by her presence. "What are you doing here?"

"We've been very busy," Zark said, puffing his chest out proudly so that steam jetted out of his nostrils, followed by a thin line of flame. "We've been flying around your world rescuing the folk the Dodman stole away from Eidolon. We've already returned half a dozen saber-toothed tigers, a baby mammoth, some satyrs, and a small stegosaurus. Then Old Creepie and his goblins got hold of our friend Zoroaster and took him through the wild road last night, so we came back to free him."

Ben repeated this for his father, and Mr. Arnold stared and stared. Then he said, "I think your friend may have already got away. Half of King Henry Close has gone up in flames and one of Aleister's neighbors babbled something about seeing a dragon come rampaging out of a truck that was parked outside. Of course, nobody believed him!" He grinned. "Well, now I have seen everything. What a wonderful story to tell your mother."

"How is she?" Ben asked anxiously.

His father frowned. "Not well." Then he smiled. "But she's very determined to come home. They said she can come out of the hospital in a day or two."

Ben breathed a sigh of relief. It was a start.

"Well, don't hang around," Zark said impatiently. He dipped a wing to Ben, who climbed carefully onto his back.

"Not too high," Ben warned.

Ishtar offered a wing to Mr. Arnold. "It would be an honor to bear the father of the Prince of Eidolon," she said.

"Eh?" said Ben's father. But, even though he could not understand the language of dragons, he climbed aboard.

"Hay is for horses!" Ben laughed; and the dragons sprang into the air and wheeled away over Aldstane Park into the first glimmering light of dawn.

# Epilogue

Two days later Ben's mother, known in one world as Mrs. Arnold and in another as Queen Isadora, returned to her family home. In her arms she carried baby Alice, and she managed for the first time in months to walk from the car right up the garden path and into the house, under the WELCOME HOME banner that Ben and Ellie had strung over the front door that very morning.

Mr. Arnold closed the door behind her. "Well,

we're all together again at last." He beamed.

Mrs. Arnold turned her face up to him for a kiss. Her cheeks were pink, Ben noticed, and her green eyes sparkled.

"Thank you, darlings," she said. "Thank you for being so brave. I know what you have done for me and," she paused, "for Eidolon."

Mr. Arnold looked at his feet, then forced a smile. Then he helped his wife to the sofa and made her a cup of tea. "Get comfortable," he said. "I have something to show you." He brought out a copy of *The Bixbury Gazette* and smoothed it flat upon the coffee table. "There," he said proudly. "Right on the front page."

## DANGEROUS ANIMAL TRADE
## RING SMASHED

ran the headline, and underneath that,

### Pet shop a front for the sale
### of illegal animals

Mr. Dodds's Pet Emporium on Bixbury High Street was yesterday the scene of a major investigation after police were tipped off by our own reporter, Clive Arnold, to the presence of certain dangerous animals being held illegally in the pet shop's stockrooms and at various private locations around the town. Police would not make details of the precise nature of their findings public, but Chief Inspector David Ramsay is quoted as saying, "Trust me, these aren't the sort of animals we want to have roaming loose on the streets of Bixbury. The consequences could be nasty. Very nasty indeed."

The creatures—including several large predators, some aquatic mammals, and what may have been a giant alligator—were being held in squalid and unsanitary conditions. Many were starving and others were almost dead from their ordeals. All those that have been recovered have now been safely rehomed, said a police spokesman, and other constabularies around the country will be mobilized to round up any animals that were sold prior to the raid.

There is currently no sign of the pet shop owner, Mr. A. E. Dodds, but police are requesting that anyone with any information as to his whereabouts contact the Bixbury Police Incident Room immediately. The public are warned not to approach him directly, since he may be armed and is to be regarded as highly dangerous.

Meanwhile, his trading partner, Mr. Aleister Creepie, has been taken into custody and is currently helping police with their inquiries. He will be charged tomorrow under twelve counts of contravening the Dangerous Animals Act. His wife Sybil (43) and daughter Cynthia (14) were taken in for questioning, but were released after a night in the cells and a great deal of complaining.

The Pet Emporium will be closed indefinitely. Chief Inspector Ramsay adds, "The police and people of Bixbury owe Mr. Arnold a debt of gratitude for his investigation into this disgraceful trade. His persistence and courage have undoubtedly saved many lives."

"The editor wrote it himself," Mr. Arnold said, "he was so pleased with the scoop. And, Izzie, he's promoted me to deputy editor!"

"Well done, Clive!" She squeezed his hand. "You are my hero."

Ben and Ellie exchanged glances. Ellie rolled her eyes. "God," she said. "If they're going to be all gooey, I'm off to watch TV."

But the story was also on the evening news, along with several reports of sightings of strange animals around the country.

"We've still got a lot of rounding up to do," said Ben. He grinned at his sister. "That'll be fun."

"Well, I'm not starting yet," Ellie said. "I'm going upstairs to do my nails."

Ben followed her up. "I'm going to play with my cat," he said.

"He's not 'your' cat," Ellie retorted.

"Well, he's certainly not yours."

"Cats belong to no one," someone said, and around the corner of Ben's bedroom door came a small black and brown cat with shiny gold eyes. It was Ignatius Sorvo Coromandel. "Though they don't mind pretending they belong to you as long as you feed them," he added hopefully.

Ben and his sister laughed.

The next morning Ben drew back his bedroom curtains and gazed out into a world that seemed to offer more hope than it had a week before. Everywhere the colors seemed just that bit brighter and the birds sang just that bit louder.

Iggy uncurled himself from where he had been sleeping at the foot of Ben's bed and came to look out of the window beside him. There was a particularly noisy blackbird chirping away on the garden gate. Iggy fixed it with a gimlet eye.

"How dare you wake me up with your racket! I'll have you," he promised, growling at it through the glass.

"I doubt that," said Ben. He tapped on the window to scare it away, but all that happened was that the bird lifted a few inches off the gate, flapped its wings wildly and fell, scrabbling from the string by which it was tethered. Ben frowned. Why would someone tie a blackbird to their garden gate?

He threw a coat on over his pajamas and ran downstairs with Ignatius Sorvo Coromandel bounding along behind him.

"Now, you're not to eat it," Ben warned the little cat. "It wouldn't be fair."

"All's fair in love and war," said Iggy cheerfully.

But it wasn't a blackbird at all. It was a mynah bird. It looked at the boy with its beady black eyes; then it looked at the cat and squawked, opening its bright orange beak wide.

"The Dodman sends his regards," it declared in an odd, mechanical fashion as if it had been taught the words by rote. "Squarrrk!"

"What?" said Ben, horrified.

"He is coming for your mother. Squarrrk! He will take her and with her power he will destroy all the magic in the world. There is nothing you can do to stop him! He will come when you least expect it, and if you get in his way, he will kill you. Squarrk!"

It cocked its head at Ben, hopped from foot to foot.

"Get this bleeding string off me, won't you, mate?" it requested. "I've done me bit now, delivered me message." It gave Iggy a hard stare with one of its shiny, orange-rimmed eyes. "Don't let that feline get me, will you, mate? I don't like the way it's lookin' at me."

"The cat won't harm you," Ben said sternly. "Tell me who gave you this message and I'll untie you."

The bird considered him, head on one side. "Well, you looks honest," it said at last. "It was Mr. Dodds himself gave me the message, and if you know the Dodman, you know he means what he says."

Ben felt a horrible wave of weariness engulf him. "Iggy, run inside and make sure my mother is safe."

The cat was gone no more than a minute. "She's asleep," he reported with a wide yawn. "As anyone sensible should be at this early hour." He fixed the mynah bird with an amber eye and the bird hopped around uncomfortably.

"Come on, mate," the mynah bird begged Ben. "Get us undone. Be fair. Don't shoot the messenger, and all that."

"Will you carry a message from me to your master?" Ben asked.

The bird fixed him with one of its beady eyes. "If you untie me I will," it promised with tremendous insincerity.

"All right, then. Tell the Dodman . . . tell him that the Prince of Eidolon sends his regards, and a warning. Tell him to leave my mother alone . . . or, or else," he finished weakly. He could not think of anything to say. "Do you understand that?"

The bird made a considering sort of noise, then repeated the message back to him, word for word.

"All right," said Ben. He undid the knotted string with which Mr. Dodds had tied the bird to the gate, and it flapped awkwardly away into the morning sky.

"Or else?" Iggy repeated derisively. "What sort of threat is that?"

He watched the bird go with narrow eyes.

"I know," said Ben with a sigh. "I couldn't think of

anything to say. Perhaps it was lying all along. Perhaps it made the whole thing up."

But in his heart he knew it hadn't. A shadow had fallen across his world again, a shadow that he hoped had somehow gone away.

"Oh, Iggy, the Dodman's been here. He's been to our house. He knows where my mother is. He's threatened to come for her. He's going to have to be stopped once and for all." Ben sat down on the grass with his head in his hands and tried to think.

"Come on," Iggy said kindly after a while, butting his head against Ben's leg. "Let's go in."

Ben attempted a smile. "Breakfast," he said, trying to sound more cheerful than he felt. "I can't think about any of this on an empty stomach."

Iggy nodded. "Food is often the best place to start."

So together the boy and the cat let themselves quietly into the kitchen of Number 27 Underhill Road and made themselves the sort of breakfast that was fit for a prince of Eidolon and a great explorer known as the Wanderer.

As they ate, they shared a thought: What in either world they would do now?

**If you enjoyed reading *The Secret Country*,
look out for the second book in the trilogy,
coming soon . . .**

The Dodman has begun his reign of terror in Eidolon. Amassing an army of trolls and giants, ghost-dogs and goblins, he is determined to lay waste to the magical Secret Country—and destroy its Queen forever.

Now Isadora must return to her world, leaving her family behind, and lead her people against the evil Dodman.

Horrified at being left behind, Ellie follows her mother to Eidolon—and walks straight into danger. Captured and held hostage by the Dodman, she can only be saved by Ben and Iggy. . . .

# About the Author

Jane Johnson was born in Cornwall and received an honors degree in English from the University of London, where —inspired by Tolkien—she specialized in Anglo-Saxon and Old Norse. After teaching drama at North London College for a year, she decided to follow up on her fascination with old Nordic language, history, and literature by getting a master's degree in Scandinavian studies at University College, a course that concentrated on the reading and translation of old Icelandic sagas. Now entirely overqualified and apparently unemployable, she was blessed by a remarkable working of fate: One day in the street she got talking to a neighbor who announced she was leaving her job. When asked where she worked, she replied, "George Allen and Unwin publishers"—magic words, since this was Tolkien's publisher. Advised to apply for the secretarial job the neighbor was vacating, (despite having no qualifications, or aptitude for secretarial work) Jane found herself, a week later, working on the Tolkien list and on Unwin's new fantasy list. Within six months she had been promoted to editor and was responsible for publishing Tolkien.

During her time at Unwin and then at HarperCollins (who took on the Tolkien list and its editor in 1990) as publishing director, she has edited and published (among many others) such diverse authors as Stephen King, Peter Straub, Dean Koontz, Clive Barker, Brian Sibley, and Arthur C. Clarke. She was also responsible for commissioning both John Howe and Alan Lee to illustrate Tolkien's works—on book covers and in calendars, and in Lee's acclaimed illustrated edition of *The Lord of the Rings*—and brought the work of Ted Nasmith to the public for the first time. The work of these three artists deeply inspired Peter Jackson in his adaptation of *The Lord of the Rings*; he took on Alan Lee as conceptual artist for the trilogy of movies and as a result Jane was invited to visit the New Zealand sets during filming of the project. She later authored the *New York Times* best-selling visual companions to the movies.

Under the names Jude Fisher and Gabriel King, Jane has written seven novels, including *The Wild Road*, *Sorcery Rising*, *Wild Magic*, and *The Rose of the World*. She lives in London with her cat and in Morocco with her husband.